A FATAL SLIP

MELISSA GLAZER

WHEELER
CHIVERS

This Large Print edition is published by Wheeler Publishing, Waterville, Maine, USA and by BBC Audiobooks Ltd, Bath, England.
Wheeler Publishing, a part of Gale, Cengage Learning.
A Clay and Crime Mystery.
The text of this Large Print edition is unabridged.
Other aspects of the book may vary from the original edition.
Set in 16 pt. Plantin.
Printed on permanent paper.

LIBRARY OF CONGRESS CATALOGING-IN-PUBLICATION DATA

Glazer, Melissa.
    A fatal slip / by Melissa Glazer. — Large print ed.
      p. cm. — (A clay and crime mystery) (Wheeler Publishing large print cozy mystery)
    Originally published: New York : Berkley Prime Crime, 2008.
    ISBN-13: 978-1-59722-963-0 (pbk. : alk. paper)
    ISBN-10: 1-59722-963-6 (pbk. : alk. paper)
    1. Potters—Fiction. 2. Vermont—Fiction. 3. Large type books.
  I. Title.
PS3607.L394F38 2009
813'.6—dc22   2009001972

BRITISH LIBRARY CATALOGUING-IN-PUBLICATION DATA AVAILABLE

Published in 2009 in the U.S. by arrangement with The Berkley Publishing Group, a member of Penguin Group (USA) Inc.
Published in 2009 in the U.K. by arrangement with The Berkley Publishing Group, a division of Penguin Group (USA) Inc.

U.K. Hardcover: 978 1 408 44154 1 (Chivers Large Print)
U.K. Softcover: 978 1 408 44155 8 (Camden Large Print)

Printed in the United States of America
1 2 3 4 5 6 7 13 12 11 10 09

For TM.
You know why, even though the world might not!

CHAPTER 1

I honestly believed that the chance to buy the building that housed my paint-your-own pottery shop, Fire at Will, was the best thing that could ever happen to me. Perched along the bank of Whispering Brook in Maple Ridge, Vermont, it was where I loved spending my days, teaching techniques in clay and how to decorate and embellish it to whoever passed through my doorway. The opportunity to own the building itself was a dream come true for me. Or so I thought. It turned out to be more of a nightmare that nearly cost me my husband, and if we're being completely honest here, my life.

It all started with an offer I couldn't refuse. No, it wasn't from the Mafia or any of their counterparts, not that we had much of an organized crime presence in Maple Ridge. I lived and worked in the quaint little town near the Green Mountains, had been married there for nearly thirty years to the same man, raising two fine sons along the way. They were the only family I knew, and we were nothing like the Corleones of *The Godfather* fame.

It really was just a good deal.

"We can do this," my husband, Bill, said as he paced around my pottery shop after hours one evening. My dear spouse was in his midfifties and was just starting to put on a little weight. He wasn't pudgy exactly, but there was certainly more to snuggle up next to on cold nights. The most striking thing about Bill was that he had the most beautiful silver hair I'd ever seen. Mine was turning a dull shade of gray, while his was becoming absolutely radiant.

As he paced, Bill said, "With my pension and what I'm bringing in from making furniture on the side, we won't have any problem with the payments if you come up short now and then."

"You're supposed to be retired, remember?" I shouldn't have had to remind him, but that was just like my husband. He'd worked as an engineer for thirty-two years, but after he'd retired, Bill had discovered that he loved making furniture — Shaker style, to be exact — and there was a real demand for it in our corner of Vermont. He'd been making pieces for Olive Haslett, owner of Shaker Styles, for years, but Bill had recently begun to branch out on his own, taking a commission here and there along with his regular work for the shop. I was happy enough with the extra money, but what really pleased me was that it gave Bill something to do while I was at Fire at Will. During his years working as an engineer, we'd dreamed about traveling in our retirement, but we'd soon discovered that we hated hotel rooms and that interstate driving gave us both a headache. Fire at Will was a way of life for me, a chance to run my own business. I was pretty good at it, too.

He grinned at me, then confirmed what I'd just been thinking. "I'm happy when I'm busy; you know that. What's holding you back? You love this place."

"I'm not denying it," I said. "But neither one of us is getting any younger."

He said sarcastically, "Well, that's a relief. Nobody else in the world has figured out how to do that, either. Carolyn, what's really the problem? You want to do this, don't you?"

"Of course I do," I finally admitted. "I just don't think it's fair to commit both of us to something that's going to have such an impact on our lives. When I started this business, we agreed that we would walk away from it anytime it got to be too much. That won't be so easy if I own the building."

He shrugged. "I've got nowhere else I'd rather be, do you?"

"That's not what I meant, and you know it. What if we decide we want to try our hand at traveling again?"

"Are you telling me you want to hit the road again?"

I shook my head. "Not like you mean. But what about a week or two at a time and not the cross-country trip we tried before? Where are we going to find the money for things like that if I've got everything tied up in Fire at Will?"

He took my hands in his, a rare romantic gesture from my normally gruff husband. "I'm happy where we are. I don't need to see the world. Where do you think you're going to find some place as beautiful as Maple Ridge?"

I glanced out at the stream near my shop. Our town had created its own version of San Antonio's River Walk a long time before anyone in Texas had even thought of it. We had a series of shops lined up neatly along

Whispering Brook, Fire at Will being one of them. A small cobblestone lane ran out front between the water and the buildings. It was indeed lovely.

"You're right, there's nowhere else I want to be either," I said. I took a deep breath, then asked, "Do you really think we should do this?"

"You're not going to get a better price, I guarantee it. Even if we change our minds later, we can sell the place for a handsome profit. I'm amazed they're letting it go for what they're asking."

"Then you don't think we should even try to haggle?"

He looked at me as if I'd slapped him. No doubt I'd offended his image of himself as the ultimate Yankee trader. "Of course we should do a little dickering. But even if they don't come down a penny, we'll still be getting a good deal. I say we jump on it."

I nodded. "I agree." The investment group that owned my building — along with several other businesses along the River Walk — had decided to unload some of their assets and were giving us, the store owners, the opportunity to buy our places first. I knew Kendra Williams had already signed the papers for her antique shop next door, Hattie's Attic, and word was Rose

Nygren, proprietress of Rose Colored Glasses, was going to follow suit. That left my own Fire at Will and In the Grounds, our coffee shop, as the only holdouts. "I'll call the management group first thing in the morning."

"Call them now before you get cold feet," Bill said, thrusting the telephone into my hand.

I took it, then put it down on the counter by the register. "Bill Emerson, I'm not going to chicken out, but I want to sleep on it before I make that kind of commitment."

"You're making a mistake," Bill said. "What if they change their minds?"

"Then it wasn't meant to be," I said. "Now let's go eat. I'm starving. Where are you taking me?"

"I thought you were buying dinner tonight," he complained.

"I cooked last night."

"You made pasta," he snapped. "How hard is it to heat up water for the noodles?"

"If it's that easy, why don't you do it yourself sometime." My husband was a whiz at making pancakes and eggs, but breakfast was about the extent of his cooking repertoire.

"No, I'll leave that to you. You want to go to Shelly's?" Shelly's Café was owned by a dear friend of mine, but I'd had lunch there already today, and I wasn't in the mood to hear Shelly proclaim to the world that I'd sold my oven and was moving into her restaurant.

"Let's go home," I said. "I'll whip something up."

"No, you don't have to do that. I'll wear a tie if I have to," Bill said reluctantly. "Where do you want to go, Andre's?" Andre's was a fancy restaurant twenty miles from Maple Ridge, the place I insisted on dining when we were celebrating every birthday, wedding anniversary, and just about any other special occasion that I could come up with when I wanted a fancy night out on the town.

"Honestly, if you can wait, I don't mind cooking. I thought a pair of pork chops would be nice, with some honeyed yams and green beans on the side. How does that sound?"

"Better than Andre's," he said. "Let's go."

"We need to stop by the grocery store on the way home."

"I don't have to go in, do I?"

"Of course you don't," I said, "though I don't know why you've got such a strong aversion to grocery shopping."

He smiled slightly. "I don't. I'm just happier waiting for you out in the parking lot."

We drove off in his truck, since we'd left my Intrigue at home when we'd made this evening excursion back to my shop. It had been a good idea to come back and remind myself exactly what I was thinking about buying, but now I needed a little time away from the place so I could make a more objective decision. Who was I trying to fool? I loved those tumbled red bricks, the emerald green awning, and even the ancient hardwood floors. I knew from the second I'd heard the offer that I was buying the place, and would have done it over my husband's protests if there had been any.

I was trying to find a nice set of pork chops in the meat department when I heard a voice right behind me that made me cringe. "Carolyn, have you made up your mind yet? What on earth are you dragging your feet for? I knew you weren't that sharp a businesswoman, but anyone can see it's the right thing to do."

"Hello, Kendra, it's nice to see you, too." What a bold-faced lie that was. Kendra Williams could be called many things, but a joy to behold was not one of them. Dressed now, as always, in a faded muumuu that had to be at least twenty years old, Kendra was the town gossip for Maple Ridge, and most days the very personal thorn in my side. I thought about asking her if she ever bought those billowing dresses brand new, but it wasn't the wisest thing in the world getting on her bad side. She could slander at the speed of light, as I had found out from a few personally unpleasant past experiences.

"Please, spare me your humor, such as it is," she said. "When are you going to sign the papers for Fire at Will?"

"Why are you so eager for me to buy my building?" I asked. "You're not getting a commission on the sale, are you?"

"Don't be ridiculous," she said.

I wasn't about to let her off the hook that easily. "Kendra, what's the catch?"

She looked up and down the grocery store aisles visible from the meat department, and when she was satisfied no one was eavesdropping on us, Kendra told me in a low voice, "You haven't talked to them yet, but I'll tell you what they're going to say. Either we all sell, or none of us gets to buy our shops."

"I thought you had a contract," I said.

"Keep your voice down. I do, but it's provisional. My lawyer told me there was nothing I could do about it, so I signed anyway. You are buying, aren't you? With the price we're getting, we'd be fools not to, and you're a lot of things, Carolyn Emerson, but I've never thought you were a fool."

Was there an actual compliment buried in there somewhere? I wasn't sure, but I wasn't going to protest the description. "I'm buying. How about Nate Walker? Have you talked to him yet?" Nate owned In the Grounds, and I couldn't imagine him just abandoning his business.

"Four or five times. Nate's still on the fence," Kendra said, frowning.

"That's odd. I thought he'd be the first one to sign up."

She shook her head. "He's afraid a national chain is going to come in and drive him out of business the second he signs the papers."

"Would they?" I knew chains had a way of wiping out small businesses, but In the Grounds had been around for twenty years, and the coffee shop appeared to have more business than any of the rest of us.

Kendra waved a meaty hand in the air. "Who knows? I can't see them coming to such a small town, but Nate's convinced the second he agrees to buy the place, the competition is going to flood in. We need to talk to him together."

"Leave me out of it," I said. "I just decided to buy Fire at Will myself. I'm not interested in pressuring him into making a decision he might regret. It took me this long to figure out that owning my place was what I wanted."

"So that gives you a vested interest in his decision. Rose and I have been talking about bracing him together, but it would be better if all three of us did it. Tomorrow at 8 A.M., I expect to see you at In the Grounds."

Before I could proclaim my reluctance again, Kendra scooted out of there like she was on wheels. I was so distracted by her determination to back Nate into a corner that I went back to the truck without another thought.

"What's wrong?" Bill asked.

"Why should something be wrong? Honestly, I don't know why you're always so negative. Can't something be right, just for once?"

"I was just curious," he said softly, "since you came out of the grocery store without any bags. Did you change your mind about dinner?"

"Of course I didn't. I just wanted to see if you'd rather have lamb chops." I was well aware that I shouldn't lie to my husband, but Kendra had flummoxed me so much that I'd completely forgotten why I'd been in the market in the first place.

"I hate lamb chops, and you know it," Bill growled.

"People change their minds all the time," I said.

"Look at me, Carolyn. Have I ever been one of those people?"

I didn't even glance over at him. "Well, if you're going to be difficult, I'll go back and get the pork chops."

He put a hand lightly on my arm. "Tell me what happened in there. You're in some kind of mood."

"We can talk about it later," I said, pulling gently away from him. "Right now I have to get us dinner. You know how grumpy you get when you don't eat on time."

"You make me sound like some kind of animal," he said.

"I don't call you an old bear for nothing," I said as I got out of the truck. As I picked up the groceries I'd need for dinner, I put a cheesecake from the bakery in my basket as well. I shouldn't have taken my aggravation with Kendra out on my husband; I knew it wasn't fair. But blast that woman, I'd just settled into the idea of owning Fire at Will, and now I was beginning to worry that the deal might not go through after all.

When I got back to the truck, this time

with two brimming grocery bags, Bill barely glanced in my direction.

"Buckle up," he snapped.

I'd hurt his feelings, that much was clear. "I didn't mean anything by what I said before."

"You call me an old bear, and you expect me to smile about it?" he asked.

"Would you rather I'd called you an old bull? How about an old goat?"

"How about not referring to me as old at all?" he suggested as he drove us home.

"Well, you're no spring chick," I said.

"In case you haven't noticed, neither are you."

"As ungracious as it is of you to remind me of that, I never claimed otherwise." I grinned over at him. "I'm still younger than you are, though."

"By seventeen months. That's not exactly a decade or two, you know."

"Believe me, I know. But it's still seventeen months."

He glanced over at me, and he must have seen my grin. "Okay, trophy wife, let's go home and eat."

After we'd had dinner, and dessert as well, Bill asked, "Are you going to tell me what upset you in the grocery store? You asked me to wait until after dinner, and I've held my tongue, but now we're finished."

"Barely," I said. "Honestly, it's not that big a deal."

"I know better than that," he said. "Tell me about it, Carolyn."

"If you must know, I ran into Kendra Williams in the meat department."

Bill nodded. "That's all you need to say. That woman could scare the paint off a barn and put a pig off its dinner."

"Don't be so dramatic. It wasn't the sight of her that upset me, it was what she said. It turns out that if we all don't buy our businesses, none of us gets the chance to own our shops."

"I thought everyone was on board with the idea," Bill said.

"From what Kendra said, it appears that Nate's still on the fence, and without In the Grounds, we all might be homeless, or at least our businesses could be."

Bill grabbed the phone, and I asked, "Who are you calling?"

"I'm going to talk some sense into Nate," he said.

I shook my head. "Bill, don't. You'll just make things worse. We're all going to talk to him tomorrow."

"Who's we?" he asked as he reluctantly

hung up the telephone.

"Kendra, Rose, and I are going by his shop together in the morning to have a word with him."

"Aren't you having coffee with Hannah?"

Hannah Atkins was my best friend as well as the mother of my assistant, David. We met every chance we got at In the Grounds for a chat and a cup of coffee before we started our days, and I missed it sorely when we went too long between get-togethers. "As a matter of fact, we're meeting with Nate an hour before Hannah and I are getting together, so I should have plenty of time."

"Are you sure you don't want me to talk to him first? I might have a little more luck than the three of you."

"What are you going to do, bully him into buying the place?"

"I resent that," my husband said darkly. "I plan to use reason with the man."

"If I need someone to reason with him that way, I'll call Butch Hardcastle." Butch was a member of the Firing Squad, a group of potters and ceramists who met once a week at Fire at Will to share new techniques for working with clay. They were also my "go-to" group whenever I got in a jam or needed help extricating myself from something unpleasant. The group included

Butch, a reformed crook; Jenna Blake, a retired judge who knew the local law enforcement community; Sandy Crenshaw, a reference librarian who could find out just about anything you'd ever need to know; and Martha Knotts, a mother of five who had more connections in Maple Ridge than the head selectman. It was an eclectic group, and I was honored to call them my friends.

"Don't call Butch. I can handle this," Bill said.

"I'm telling you, I don't need either one of you. I can take care of this myself."

"So let me get this straight. You'll take help from Kendra and Rose, but not from me or the rest of your gang? You know that doesn't make any sense, don't you?"

"I don't have to make sense, I'm your wife," I said.

He shook his head in mock disgust — at least I hoped he was faking it — and went into the living room to watch *MythBusters,* his favorite television show. Usually I watched with him, but I figured I'd had enough stimulation for one day and decided to skip tonight's episode. I sat out on the back porch and stared at the woods behind our house, though their beauty was lost on me at the moment. There had to be some way to convince Nate that the town of Maple Ridge needed him and his coffee shop, and I wondered if I could prove my earnestness to him without sounding like I had too much of a vested interest in the outcome of his decision.

"Where's Rose? Did you remember to tell her to meet us here?" Kendra and I were standing outside In the Grounds the next morning much too early, at least in my opinion.

"She'll be here," Kendra said. "Why are you suddenly in such a hurry to speak with Nate?"

I wrapped my coat around me as I said, "I don't care if it is nearly June; it's freezing this morning." While our late spring days were rarely what anyone would call tropical, we were generally a few shades warmer than this. I'd somehow missed glancing at the thermometer before I'd left the house, but one step outside and I knew I had to have a jacket. I was beginning to wish that I'd dug a little deeper in my closet for something warmer than the windbreaker I was wearing. "Let's go inside and get some coffee, then we can come back out here and wait for Rose."

"We'll do no such thing," Kendra commanded. "We will go in strong and all together. It's the only way to appear with a show of force."

I tried to keep my teeth from chattering as I asked, "What force are we trying to show? We don't have the least bit of power or influence here. If Nate doesn't want to buy the shop, there's nothing we can do to convince him otherwise."

"Don't sell the power of three independent women acting together short, Carolyn. You've been married too long if you've forgotten what a formidable foe a woman can be."

"I tend to think of my marriage as more of a partnership than a war zone, Kendra." The woman had some kind of nerve.

"Then perhaps that's where you've erred in your life."

Okay, that was just about all the snootiness I was going to take from her. "And exactly how long have you ever been married at one time to the same man? You don't have to give me the longest one, just try to come up with a cumulative total for your last three husbands," I said, my biggest fake smile plastered on my face. It was a mean thing to say, but she'd asked for it. Well, she had. Okay, maybe the chilly temperature and my need for a caffeine fix had driven me beyond the boundaries of propriety, but that was just too bad.

"I've been married only twice, and you know it. I don't care to tabulate the years in my life I have wasted on men," Kendra said. "Nor should you."

"Hey, I never said I wasted a minute of my life being married to Bill." This conversation had the potential to get really ugly really fast.

Fortunately, Rose showed up before Kendra and I could square off in the street for some hand-to-hand combat.

Kendra saved me from snapping at Rose for being late by beating me to the punch. "Did your clocks all fail on you this morning?"

Rose blushed, turning her normally pale complexion the same shade of red as her hair. "I'm sorry. I had company last night."

"Was it IBM or Xerox?" I asked, smiling.

"What? No, not that kind of company. I meant I had a visitor. A man," she added lamely.

"And when did he leave?" Kendra asked as she studied Rose with those hawklike eyes. "Or is he still at your house waiting impatiently for your return?"

"He's not there now," Rose said, and if anything, her blush deepened. The poor girl needed rescuing, but I wasn't in the mood to do the honors. Maybe that would teach her not to keep her friends waiting for her while she was off dallying with a new man. Did I actually just think that? Where had my spirit gone? Could Kendra be right? Maybe I was just an old married woman after all. But was there anything wrong with that? It surely beat Kendra's lifestyle, and Rose's, too, for that matter. No, with all his faults, and trust me, Bill had more than his share, I was certainly happier with him than I would have been without him, and in the end, that was the only thing that mattered.

I'd had just about enough of Kendra's browbeating. "Leave her alone, Kendra."

Rose glanced at me with her obvious thanks, but I wasn't about to let her off the hook that easily. "She's right, though. You did keep us waiting."

"I said I was sorry."

"Don't keep apologizing, just get some coffee in me. We can surely take enough time for a cup before we brace Nate."

Kendra scowled. "I agree with Shake-speare's sentiment that if there's something unpleasant to be done, it is best done quickly."

"And I agree with Juan Valdez. There's always time for a cup of coffee. Besides, it will remind Nate that not only are we his fellow business owners, but we're his customers, too."

"She's got a point," Rose said, backing me up.

Kendra was wavering; I could see it in her eyes. It was time to push her over the edge. "Tell you what. The coffees are on me, and I don't even mind if you get that expensive blend you love so much. Come on."

"Very well, if you two insist," she finally said.

It was all the encouragement I needed. I was at the counter in front ordering before Rose and Kendra even made it through the door. After we placed our orders and I was paying, I asked the man behind the counter, "Is Nate around?"

"He didn't come in this morning," the clerk said.

"Is he sick?" I had never been in the coffee shop when Nate wasn't somewhere on the premises.

"Not that I know of," he said as he gave me my change. "He's the boss. He doesn't have to ask me for permission for a day off if he feels like taking one. Next."

I stood my ground, ignoring the push from behind from a fresh batch of customers. "This is important."

"Then call him at home, if you want to risk getting your head bit off. Nate doesn't like to talk business when he's away from the shop. Excuse me, but there's a line of folks behind you."

There was no excuse for him, but I stepped aside anyway. Kendra and Rose were sitting at a table by the window when I carried the tray with our coffees over to them.

As I passed them out, I said, "He's not here. The clerk told me Nate's taking the day off."

Kendra stood. "That's impossible. He never takes a vacation. If these doors are open, he's here."

"That's what I thought, but the clerk didn't agree."

"We'll just see about that," Kendra said as she stormed toward the counter.

Rose asked, "Should we go with her?"

"Are you kidding? I'm sure we'll be able to hear every word she says. Besides, I want to sit here and enjoy my coffee, don't you?"

"I could use the jolt," Rose admitted.

I took a sip, then asked, "So, who's your mystery man?" As her cheeks blossomed again, I added, "Rose, you really are going to have to learn to control that."

She touched her face with her hands. "It's

just awful, isn't it? I hate it when I blush. I think of it as the curse of the redhead."

"Then try not to think about it. Let's see, what might take your mind off it? I know. Tell me who was at your place until all hours of the morning."

Rose shook her head, though she still couldn't control the blush of her cheeks. "I'm not saying," she said. "I don't want to jinx it."

"Then don't tell Kendra," I said. "She'll have it all over town by lunch. Speak of the devil and she appears," I added as Kendra rejoined us.

"Ladies, we're leaving."

I still had half a cup left, and she hadn't touched hers yet. "Can't we at least finish drinking our coffee first?"

"There's no time for that. Bring them."

As I grabbed my coat, I asked, "Where exactly are we going in such a hurry?"

Kendra said, "We're going to find the errant coffeehouse owner. I have a sneaking suspicion where he's hiding from us."

"Who said he was hiding?" I asked. "He didn't even know we were coming by."

"Believe me, if I know Nate Walker — and I do — there's no doubt about it, I know exactly where he'll be."

I wasn't sure I really wanted to know, but

there was something in me that made me ask. "Kendra, where exactly are we going?"

"To the cemetery."

CHAPTER 2

"He's not here. Can we go back to the coffee shop and wait for him there?" Rose asked Kendra in a whining voice. The town cemetery, filled with tombstones that ranged from the seventeen hundreds to just a few weeks old, looked brooding and forlorn, even with the weak sunshine trying to break through the clouds.

"Don't be such a baby. I know Nate's around here somewhere. We saw his van in the parking lot, didn't we?"

"I hate this place," Rose said as she kept glancing around. "It always gives me the shivers."

"How about you, Carolyn?" Kendra asked me as she arched one eyebrow. "Are you frightened of cemeteries as well?"

"I'm not in any hurry to take up residence in one, but they don't bother me otherwise. I have too many old friends and family buried here. What made you think that Nate came here? It's not where most folks would spend a rare day off, is it?"

Kendra shrugged. "I was here a few months ago and saw him kneeling beside one of the graves. A caretaker told me he visits the site often, and I made a mental note of it. Look, there he is, over by the maple tree."

I looked where she was pointing, and sure enough, Nate Walker was leaning over a grave site, having what appeared to be an earnest conversation with whoever was in residence there.

"Shouldn't we give him some privacy?" I asked. "I hate to intrude on him."

Kendra snapped, "He's not hosting a party, Carolyn. We need to talk to him, and we can't put it off. Don't tell me you're getting cold feet."

"They would match the rest of me, since I'm still freezing, but no, I want to own Fire at Will, if there's any way possible to do it."

She nodded in triumph. "Then let's go see if we can make it happen. Come on."

Neither Rose nor I had any real choice in the matter. We followed Kendra as she bore down on Nate with a stoked fire in her steps. I felt sorry for the coffee shop owner, but at least Kendra's determination wasn't focused on me, and that was something to be grateful for. I'd been the target of her powerful personality too many times before.

Nate looked shocked to find us approaching him at the grave site. He mumbled something to the stone, then stood and met us a ways from the interment, as if he were shielding the conversation from the occupant. "What are you three doing here?" he asked in a hushed voice.

"We need to talk to you," Kendra said in a reply that disregarded Nate's tone. "It's about the coffee shop."

"I don't want to talk about it right now," Nate said. There was nothing unsure in his voice.

I touched Kendra's arm. "Come on. Let's do this later."

"We'll do it now," she said harshly.

"I said no," Nate said as he started to walk past us.

Kendra stepped in front of him to block off his escape. "Have you made up your mind, then?"

She wasn't backing down, and we had no choice but to stand together. All three of us looked at him earnestly. He took his time replying, then said, "So that's what this is about. You're concerned that I'm going to blow the sale for the three of you." Nate looked at me with his piercing blue eyes.

"Now you're in on it, too?"

"It's true that I want to buy the pottery shop," I said, trying to at least make my voice match his. "Is that so wrong?"

His angular face softened. "Of course not. I'm just not sure I can go through with it."

Kendra said, "So you're going to sink us as well. I've known you practically all your life, flaws and features through and through, but I never took you as someone so selfish."

He looked at her with a fierce expression in his eyes, and I saw his hands ball up into fists. "You know I'm not. I just haven't made up my mind yet. Don't push me."

"Leave him alone, Kendra," Rose said. She'd moved away from us and was staring down at the tombstone Nate had just been visiting.

"Get away from there," Nate said sharply when he noticed where she was standing.

Rose looked at him as if he'd slapped her. "I'm sorry. I didn't mean . . . I was just trying . . . I'm so sorry." She ran back toward town — a thousand yards from the cemetery — and I started to follow her.

"Where are you going?" Kendra asked me acidly.

"I'm going to see if I can comfort her." Before I left, I turned to Nate and added, "You didn't have to be that mean to her.

What's gotten into you?"

He didn't answer, and honestly, the man looked as surprised by the outburst as Rose had been. At the moment, I didn't care about him, or Kendra, either. All I wanted was to catch up with Rose and offer her some aid, if I could.

I found her in Rose Colored Glasses. Her shop was full of stained glass objects, from bird feeders to sun catchers, and the predominant color scheme was red. I knew when I was upset, Fire at Will was where I wanted to be. There, or home, but then again, I had Bill waiting for me there. I wasn't sure what or whom Rose had waiting on her, but she'd headed to her shop, so that had to say something about her current disposition.

I found her dabbing at her cheeks when I walked in. "Hey, it's all right. He didn't mean anything by it."

She looked at me with red eyes. "Do you think I ran in here because my feelings were hurt? I'm tougher than that, Carolyn."

"Then what happened?"

"You didn't see the tombstone, did you?"

"No, I didn't get the chance. Who was it, one of his parents?"

"It was worse than that. It was his wife."

"I should have guessed as much."

Rose looked confused. "I didn't realize Nate had ever been married."

"That's right, you came to town a few years after it happened. I remember it all too well. Winnie and Nate Walker had only been married three years when she died."

Rose looked stricken. "What happened to her? Was it cancer or something like that?"

"No, she was killed by a hit-and-run driver one night after locking up the coffee shop by herself. Nate had been home sick, and when he hadn't heard from her, he dragged himself out of bed in the middle of the night to look for her. I heard that the shock of finding her lifeless body crumpled by the side of the road nearly killed him."

"How horrible it must have been." Rose looked as though she was going to weep again.

"It's been fifteen years, but I don't doubt Nate still mourns for her. As far as I know, he's never even looked at another woman since then. To make matters worse, they never did find the driver who struck her, and long after the police gave up, Nate did his best to find her killer himself."

"Did he?"

"No, I think he finally realized it wasn't going to happen."

"It's absolutely tragic, isn't it?"

Rose had a tendency to state the obvious, but I had to agree with her. "I've always felt bad for Nate."

Rose finished dabbing her cheeks. "Kendra just made things worse, didn't she?"

"That's what she does," I said, rather uncharitably.

"Do you think it's a lost cause?"

"No, I just think we need to take a different approach."

Rose looked me in the eye. "What are you going to do?"

"I'm going to talk to Nate alone and see if I can help him make his decision."

"Don't push him too hard."

"Don't worry," I said as I walked to the door. "I'll push just enough."

Nate was back at the coffee shop standing behind the counter as if nothing had happened when I walked in. When I approached him, I said, "Sorry about that."

"You don't have anything to apologize for," Nate replied, with more than a touch of frost in his voice.

"I'm asking for forgiveness collectively, since I doubt Kendra's going to do it."

That broke a slight crack in his dour expression. "It would be eventful, wouldn't it?"

"I'd say practically apocalyptic, wouldn't you?"

"That works." He frowned, then added, "I'm sorry about the way I reacted out there. Is Rose all right?"

"She's fine now. We should have given you some privacy," I said. "I'm sorry we ganged up on you like that."

"Not a problem. Would you like some coffee?"

I'd just had one cup and was going to have another one with Hannah soon, but I couldn't exactly turn him down. "Sure, why not? Is there any chance you'd join me?"

I didn't think I had a prayer of succeeding, but to my surprise, he agreed. "I could use a little warming up myself. Find us a table and I'll be right there."

He joined me a minute later and put a giant mug in front of me. "I figured you could use a bigger jolt than you're used to."

"Sounds great," I said as I took a sip. After a moment, I asked, "Would you like to talk about it?"

"What, the weather, or the chances the Red Sox have this year?"

I shook my head. "You're as bad as Bill. You know exactly what I mean."

He shrugged. "There are worse things than being compared to your husband. He's a good guy."

"I think so, too, but sometimes I wonder. Answer me, Nate, and stop avoiding the topic."

"I wasn't exactly sure we'd settled on one yet." He took a sip of his own coffee, and a slight smile slipped out.

"You're a big fan of your product, aren't you?"

"Aren't you?"

I nodded. "I guess all of our businesses start out of a love for what we do."

He smiled softly as he stared into his cup. "Not me." He glanced around the shop, then said wistfully, "This place was always Winnie's dream, not mine."

I had to choose my next words carefully. "And yet you've kept it going all these years."

"Silly, isn't it? I guess I believe as long as the business stays open, a little of my wife will still be around."

I patted his hand. "I don't think that's silly at all. Tell me how you got started. I didn't have my pottery shop back then, so I wasn't as tied to the River Walk as I am now."

"We met in college," Nate said. "It was love at first sight, at least for me. It took Winnie some time to come around, but I finally wore her down. She wanted a coffee shop more than anything else in the world."

"How about you?"

"I wanted her to be happy. We could have had a flower shop or a bowling alley for that matter. All I cared about was being with her."

"You must miss her terribly," I said.

"Every day." He looked around In the Grounds, then said, "It's a horrid name, but she was dead set on it, and I didn't put up much of a fight. Carolyn, maybe it's time I let go."

"Maybe you're right," I said. Sure, it would sting if I lost Fire at Will, but Nate had a lot more at stake than I did.

He looked surprised by my agreement. "You wouldn't hate me if I decided not to buy this place?"

"Of course not," I said, meaning every word of it. "I'll respect whatever decision you make. No matter what you decide, though, you should get on with your life. If that means shutting this place down and doing something else, I'm sure Winnie would have approved."

"She wanted me to be happy," he said. The poor man appeared to be on the brink of tears. Was it something I was doing? First Rose, and now Nate.

There was only one piece of advice I could

give him. "Then you should follow your heart."

"Thanks," Nate said as he squeezed my hand. Wiping an errant tear from his cheek, he said with false heartiness, "Now I've dawdled too long. It's time to get back to work."

After he was back at the counter, I took one more sip of coffee, then I headed for the door, nearly knocking Hannah down as I did so.

"Were you giving up on me already?" she said. Hannah glanced at her watch. "I'm only three minutes late."

"Come on," I said as I reversed direction. "Let me buy you a cup of coffee."

"It's my turn to treat, remember?" she said. Hannah, a slim brunette barely over forty, was an English professor at Travers College.

"Fine, but I think I'd like a hot chocolate instead."

"No coffee? Are you sure?" She looked at me as if I'd lost my mind. "You always need an early morning pick-me-up."

"A woman can change her mind occasionally, can't she?" I wasn't in the mood to admit that I was already nearing a caffeine overdose.

"Hot chocolate it is. In fact, it's so chilly

out today, I think I'll join you."

As we sipped our hot cocoas, Hannah asked, "Is there something wrong?"

"You mean besides the usual sea of troubles that seems to surround me?"

"Don't be flip," she said. "I'm here, if you need someone to talk to."

I nodded. "Thanks, I appreciate that." I glanced back at Nate, who was studiously cleaning the counter between orders. "It's nothing I can talk about. At least not here," I said as I lowered my voice.

Hannah looked around. "You can whisper if you'd like. Is it about someone in here?" She glanced around the room. "I know. It's about Dawn's new perm, isn't it? Normally I don't like to gossip, but what was that woman thinking?"

I looked at Dawn Houser, a woman who had been friends with my mother, and marveled at her new hairstyle. There wasn't a name for the color of her frosted tresses, but the closest I could come to it was a light purple with tinges of burgundy. "It's amazing what they can do with chemicals these days. But no, that's not it. Do you have time to walk me to my shop?"

She looked at her watch. "I've got an early class, but I could always call my TA and let her get things started."

Hannah would do it, I knew that, but she'd be committing a serious dereliction of duty if she foisted off work on her assistant when she was capable of teaching herself. "I know you better than that. Go on. We'll catch up later."

As we walked outside, she said, "I mean it. I want a rain check."

"You've got it."

As I walked toward Fire at Will, I dreaded the prospect of running into either Kendra or Rose, but for once, luck was with me and I got to my place unscathed.

David, my twenty-year-old, ponytailed assistant, was standing inside the shop when I walked in.

"Good morning," I said as I hung up my jacket on one of the pegs in back and reached for an apron.

"I've just heard the news," he said. "You're not buying the shop, are you? Carolyn, how can you do this to me?"

As I tied my apron around my waist, I said, "I didn't realize I was doing anything to you. It's my shop and my decision." To placate his scowl, I added, "Besides, you've gotten your facts mixed up. I'm making an offer as soon as we're finished with this inane conversation."

"I just heard . . . Someone at Shelly's say

that you were holding out from the rest of the group."

"Do you happen to remember who you heard it from?" Honestly, it was bad enough taking the hits around town for the things I actually did, but that wasn't good enough for the local rumor mill. It seemed that if there wasn't anything worth talking about, they'd just started making things up.

"I didn't really hear who said you weren't buying the place," he admitted. "So it's not true?"

"If you don't believe me, you can listen in on the phone conversation."

I dialed the number I'd been given. "I need to speak with Melody Train, please."

"One moment, please." I was quickly connected, then identified myself. "I'm interested in purchasing the building where my shop, Fire at Will, is located," I said, my voice quivering a little.

"Wonderful, Ms. Emerson. Now, you should know that this offer is conditional on all shop owners buying their respective buildings?"

"Yes, I had heard that. I understand. I'm curious about one thing, though."

"Why are you getting such a great price?" I could almost hear the smile in her voice.

"That's it exactly. I don't mean to look a

gift horse in the mouth and all of that, but I couldn't help wondering."

"I don't blame you a bit. The owners want to liquidate as quickly as possible, and they're not exactly hurting for a cash influx at the moment. To be honest with you, I've been surprised you all haven't acted quicker, before they change their minds."

"There's no danger of that, is there?" Suddenly the thought of losing Fire at Will was more than I could take.

"No, as long as you all agree. We have one more party to sign, and then we'll be able to act quickly. I'll send the paperwork around to your shop by the end of the day, if that's all right."

I remembered Nate's reluctance earlier and wondered if I was wasting my time, but he hadn't definitely said no yet, and if he did decide to buy In the Grounds, I wanted to be ready for it. "That would be great."

"Thanks for calling," she said.

As I hung up, David's smile broadened.

"Don't get too excited," I warned him. "We still need Nate Walker at In the Grounds."

"He'll sign up for sure," David said.

"There's nothing sure about it. Now let's get a little work done before a mad horde of customers rushes in here."

"Are you expecting anybody in particular to come in today?"

"No, but I can hope, can't I? What's next on your dream list of things to try?" My assistant, as well as being a part-time student at Travers, also had the most outlandish wish list of pottery projects I'd ever seen.

"Medusa masks," he said with a gleam in his eye.

"Do I even want to know?"

"Come on, it will be fun."

As we wedged fresh clay side by side, working out the air bubbles and smoothing it, I said, "You seem to be building more pieces by hand lately. Have you sworn off throwing on the wheel?"

"No, I still like to throw, but I'm enjoying this process. You know how I got interested in it?"

"Let me guess. You saw a Rodin exhibit?"

"No, I saw a face jug from North Carolina. Robert Owens has been making them at the school, and they looked intriguing."

Owens was a part-time pottery instructor at the shop, though he was becoming less and less a presence at Fire at Will. Between his regular classes at Travers and his extra-curricular student activities — and by that I meant running after coeds — he didn't have much time for my little pottery shop any-more.

"I've seen them." Face jugs were regular thrown pots, with the addition of eyes, teeth, ears, and a nose.

He nodded. "I know, they can be an acquired taste, but they are folk art at its best. I was making noses and eyes, and I started thinking of the other possibilities."

"So, let's make a few face jugs instead."

"We can later, but I want to do these masks first."

My clay was ready. "That suits me. Should we make the first one together, or should we work separately?"

"Let's do the first one together. I'll work on the mask, and you start on some snaky hair."

We worked our balls of clay down to sheets a quarter of an inch thick. French rolling pins were the best for that job, and David and I had each done enough that we didn't need spacers to tell us when we got down to the right thickness.

"That's easy enough." As David cut the basic shape of the mask from his rolled sheet of clay, I started cutting mine into inch-wide strips. After I'd fashioned a series of pencil-thick strands, I sculpted snake heads at each end, including the addition of hissing tongues.

David looked at one. "Wow, you're really good at this."

"What can I say, I've met more than my share of snakes in my life. I just did these from memory."

By the time I had a few dozen snakes formed, David was ready with the mask head. "May I?"

"Be my guest."

I watched as he scored the forehead of the mask with several crisscross lines, then did the same on the ends of the snake bodies. After dabbing a brush into some liquid clay slip and coating both surfaces, David worked the first snake into position. He moved quickly, and soon the head of snake hair was in place.

"Now for the eyes," he said as he took an X-Acto knife and cut out the openings. In twenty minutes, he'd added a nose and full lips to the mask.

"She's great, isn't she?" he asked.

"I'd hate to be her beautician," I said.

David set it aside. "Are you ready to do your own?"

"Why not? It might add a little flair to our display window." Or it might drive folks off. I'd wait to see how the masks turned out glazed before I made any decisions.

We were just about to tackle our solo masks when the front door chimed. I was surprised to see that it was Nate Walker.

"Carolyn, do you have a second?"

"Sure. Just let me wash up." As I was drying my hands, I told David, "I'll be up front if you need me."

"Fine," he said, though I doubted he'd heard me. David had a tendency to focus solely on the task at hand, no matter what that might be. There was a spark of genius in him, but it wasn't just his talent. It was that ability he had to concentrate to the exclusion of everything else. I envied his focus but knew I could never come close to matching it. I was too easily distracted by the world around me.

"What can I do for you, Nate?"

"I've made my decision about In the Grounds, and I thought you should be the first one to know."

I knew in my heart that he'd decided not to accept the offer, but I couldn't bring myself to try to change his mind, no matter how much I personally would lose. My business was my present, but his was his past. If he needed to close the coffee shop in order to get on with his life, I wouldn't get in his way. I'd find another location for Fire at Will, though I'd miss looking out at Whispering Brook every day.

"Go ahead," I said, preparing myself for the worst.

"I'm buying in, too."

"I understand," I said before the words hit home. "What did you just say?"

"I'm staying," he said with a grin. "In the end, when it came down to it, I just couldn't bear to leave the place."

"Don't get me wrong, I'm thrilled, but I thought there were too many ghosts there for you."

He took my hands in his. "Carolyn, I think ghosts have gotten a bad reputation. What's wrong with having memories of Winnie wherever I look? I loved my wife. We had too many good times together to ever forget. She poured her life into that shop, and I'm going to keep it afloat just as long as I can."

"But you were so worried about the competition moving in on your business," I said.

"Carolyn, don't you want me to stay?"

"Of course I do. I just want you to make the decision for the right reasons." Honestly, he was on the money. What was I trying to do, talk him out of this? Still, when it came down to it, I wanted my shop, but not at Nate's expense.

"I am. Do you happen to have the owner's

number? I'd like to get this moving."

I dug into my pocket, since I'd been carrying the contact information around with me since I'd decided buying in myself. "It's right here. You can use my phone, if you'd like."

"Thanks, but this is one call I want to make from In the Grounds. It's probably silly, isn't it?"

"Not at all. I'm so happy, Nate. Thank you."

"I should be the one thanking you. You never put a bit of pressure on me, and I want you to know how much I appreciate it."

It was a good thing the man couldn't read my thoughts, or he never would have made the deal. "Shall I tell the others?"

"Not right away. Let's make them sweat a little." His smile was brighter than I had seen it in years.

"You're wicked, you know that, don't you?"

"You have no idea. In fact, I think I'm going to stop by Kendra's and tell her I've nearly made up my mind and it doesn't look good."

I laughed. "That's just pure evil. Can I tag along? I want to see her face."

"Now who's evil?"

"We both are," I said. "I really am happy about your decision."

"So am I."

After he was gone, I called Bill and told him the good news.

His response was to the point. "Did you call the sellers yet?"

"Yes, this morning, but I'll have to call them back now that Nate's in. Are you sure this is what you want to do? It's your last chance to back out."

"You mean it's yours. Call them, Carolyn."

"Fine." I hung up on him, then dialed Melody's number again. I was told that as soon as Nate confirmed my story, the final papers, not the preliminary ones that Rose and Kendra had signed, would be delivered by courier for my signature, and my down payment would be required as well. It looked as though I'd just bought myself a pottery studio. My hands were shaking as I wrote out the check, but in a good way. I was on my way to owning my dream, and it appeared that nothing was going to stop it now.

At least I hoped that was the way it was going to turn out.

CHAPTER 3

"Charlie Cobb, you are a pigheaded fool," my husband shouted in the back room of Fire at Will a week later.

"I won't stand for that kind of talk, Bill Emerson, and you know it. You'll either do it my way, or you won't do it at all."

At least I didn't have any customers at the moment, and closing time was just thirty minutes away. We'd signed the papers for the shop with alacrity, and before I knew what was happening, the building was mine. Bill and I had decided that no matter how tight it squeezed us, there were some changes we had to make now that Fire at Will was ours. Well, ours and the bank's.

"Do you two need a time-out?" I asked as I walked to the back of the shop.

"Carolyn, stay out of this," Bill said.

"It's her building," Charlie said. "She's entitled to an opinion. It's got to be worth more than yours."

53

"Don't start with me," Bill said.

"You know what? You're right." He got out some paperwork, wrote a few things, then stamped something on the sheet. Even without my glasses, I had no trouble making out the stop-work order as he tacked it to the wall of what was going to be my new bathroom.

"Wait a second, there's no need to be hasty," I said. "Surely there's a way we can work this out."

"You have two choices. You can comply with my order, or you can sell this place and move," Charlie said.

"Now are you ready for me to tell you what you can do?" Bill growled.

"Bill. Leave. Please." I added the last bit as my husband directed his glare to me.

He scowled at Charlie a second, and I could tell he was getting ready to fire another volley at the man. I quickly stepped between them and whispered to him, "Don't make this any worse than it already is."

Instead of an answer, he grunted, but to my husband's credit, he did exactly as I asked and walked out of the shop.

Charlie was still writing something on his clipboard when I turned to him. In my gentlest voice, I asked, "Now, can we talk about this like two rational adults?"

"The time for talking is over. If you don't agree with my order, you can always appeal it."

"To Pete Young? You're kidding, right?" Pete ran the building inspection department for Maple Ridge, and he was known unaffectionately around town as Pucker-Up Pete. The man would say no to his mother, if she were ever foolish enough to give him the chance, and it appeared that Charlie was following closely in his mentor's footsteps.

"Mr. Young is my supervisor, and I'd appreciate it if you would treat him with respect."

This was getting me nowhere. "I'm sorry. Charlie, I need this bathroom. As it is, I barely have running water in the place." Bill and I had decided to save some money by redoing the bathroom ourselves. My husband had put his latest furniture order on hold and had gleefully ripped out the old sink and toilet. He'd been in the process of expanding the bathroom's narrow confines when Charlie had gotten wind of our remodeling. We hadn't even realized we'd need a permit to start moving walls and fixtures around, but evidently the building code for our little Vermont town was taken straight from Big Brother's manual on harassing do-it-yourselfers. We were in an historic district that took the town's bylaws rather seriously, and I was beginning to see the world through the eyes of an owner instead of a renter.

"I can't help that," Charlie said. "It's not my problem."

"What can I do?" I was frantic about solving this.

"You can get a permit. Until then, I'd advise you to do as I say and stop this construction."

"How long does it take to get a permit?" I imagined running home every time I had to go to the bathroom, not a pleasant thought at all, and I didn't even want to think about what I would do with my customers. Would I have to send them to Kendra? What a headache.

Charlie said, "It takes as long as it takes."

He left, and I was getting ready to lock the shop so I could go after the coveted permit when I heard shouting out front.

Bill hadn't gone far, and it appeared that he and Charlie had moved right into Round Two.

"You're not going to get away with this," Bill shouted at Charlie. Their noses were barely six inches apart as they screamed.

"Look around. I already did. That permit's

going to be stuck in molasses, and you better believe it." It was pretty clear that Charlie was just as mad as Bill.

"If I can't go around you, then I'll go straight through you," my husband shouted at him.

I had to stop this. There was only one thing to do. I forced myself between them and turned my back to Charlie so I could face Bill. "Go home."

"But —"

"Go home," I repeated. There was not a whisper of love or affection in my voice as I said it.

Bill turned and stormed off, and before I could apologize to Charlie yet again, he left as well. There was quite a crowd gathered along the River Walk, and I could only imagine how fast the story of the fight would spread through Maple Ridge.

I wanted to crawl back into the shop and lock the door behind me, but I knew that wasn't the way to deal with the situation. No matter how unpleasant it was, I had to walk to the town hall and file the papers for that permit right now. Otherwise I was going to have to put a Porta Potti in back of the shop, and I knew that wouldn't exactly entice new customers into the place.

■ ■ ■ ■

Of course, the building inspection department was closed for the day. I had to
wonder if Charlie had planned his visit to
throw the maximum amount of chaos our
way. There had been bad blood between
him and my husband for years, over a
softball game, of all things. Fifteen years
before, Bill had been a pitcher for the Ridge
Runners, and Charlie had been at bat for
the Dirt Devils. Bill's slow pitch had inadvertently beaned Charlie in the head, knocking off his batter's helmet and sending him
to the ground. To my husband's credit, he'd
tried to apologize, but the pitch had nearly
cleared both benches. That was my husband's last foray into sports, but Charlie
had never accepted the fact that the pitch
had *accidentally* hit his head. At least, Bill
had sworn it was an errant pitch. Now, I
knew my husband's temper better than
anyone else in the world, and even I wasn't
sure it had *really* been an accident.

I stared at the glass door of the inspector's
office, but wishing didn't open it, so I
decided to go home. This problem would
have to wait until tomorrow.

Bill wasn't at the house when I got home,

58

but I found a message for me on our machine. "Carolyn, I'm going to make up some time working on this nightstand, so don't wait up."

That was certainly short and to the point. There was one more message on my machine, and I heard my husband's voice again. "Didn't mean to lose my cool today. I need to blow off some steam. I'll grab something later, so go ahead and eat."

I'd picked up some ground turkey for dinner, but there was no way I was making my famous patties just for me. Then I had a thought.

I picked up the phone and dialed Hannah's number. "Hey, it's me."

"Hey, me, what's going on?"

"Bill stood me up for dinner, and I was wondering if you'd like to grab a bite with me tonight."

She chuckled. "What, kind of like a ladies' night out? It's pretty short notice."

"Sorry, I should have known you'd have plans. We'll do it another time."

Hannah said, "Wait a second, I didn't say I was busy. What did you have in mind?"

"Well, we could go to Shelly's, or I could make something for us here."

She didn't even have the grace to hesitate before she said, "I choose Shelly's."

"Gee, thanks. I thought you liked my cooking."

"That's not it. I've been struggling with creating a new test all afternoon, and it might be fun to get out in the world."

"I thought the students had trouble with tests, not the teachers."

She sighed. "You'd think so, but can you imagine how hard it is to make up a test that's fair yet challenging enough to reward those who've been paying attention all semester? I wrestle with it every term."

"You mean you don't use the same test every time you teach the course?"

Hannah chuckled again. "No, my students are far too industrious for that. I don't want anyone with access to earlier exams to get a free pass. Do you want me to pick you up, or should we meet at Shelly's?"

"Let's meet there. See you in ten minutes."

After I hung up, I tried calling Bill at Olive's workroom in town, but there was no answer. I wasn't surprised. Between the power tools he used and the ear plugs he wore for protection, he wouldn't have been able to hear a jumbo jet flying overhead let alone the phone ringing. In case he came home without checking his messages, I left him a note, then took off for Shelly's.

The café's namesake was working the grill when I walked in. Shelly was a petite woman, but her small stature belied a biting wit that could draw blood. Fortunately, I rarely saw her fangs, since we'd been friends close to forever.

"Hey," I greeted her, then suspecting she might comment on Bill's absence, I quickly added, "Before you say a word about me being here alone, I'm meeting Hannah Atkins."

Shelly ignored my comment and motioned for me to come closer, then asked, "Rose Nygren is a friend of yours, isn't she?"

"I guess you could say that," I admitted. "Why?"

Shelly gestured to the back of the café, and I saw Rose sitting in a booth by herself. From the redness in her eyes, it looked as though she'd been crying.

Shelly asked, "Could you talk to her? I tried, but she blew me off."

"Sure," I said. "Any idea what's going on?"

"Not a clue."

As I approached Rose, she looked startled to see me. I asked gently, "Can I join you? It'll just be for a second. I'm meeting somebody."

"I don't know," Rose said as she dabbed

at her eyes with a napkin. "I was just leaving."

"Hang around a second, okay?" I slid into the booth, then put my hand on hers. "Rose, are you all right?"

"Why? What have you heard?"

"It doesn't take a detective to see that you're upset. If you want to talk about it, I'm here for you."

Rose took a deep breath, then said, "He dumped me. Can you believe it? He got what he wanted, then he threw me away like yesterday's trash. I'm such a fool. I believed him."

"It's not your fault," I said. "We can't always control what our hearts do, or the people we choose to trust with them."

"He used me," she said softly.

"Who are we talking about?" I didn't mean to pry, but it might help if I knew who we were talking about.

Rose was about to tell me — I could see the answer in her eyes — when Hannah approached. "Hey, you two. Can I join you?"

"I was just leaving," Rose said as she slid out of the booth.

"You don't have to go on my account," Hannah said.

"Yes, please, stay," I added.

Rose wasn't interested, though. "No,

thanks." She threw a ten at Shelly, then bolted from the café.

"What was that all about?" Hannah asked. "Did I interrupt something?"

I couldn't very well tell her that she had, though I wished her timing had been a little better. "Apparently Rose just got dumped."

"I'm so sorry," Hannah said. "I didn't even realize she was dating anyone. Did you happen to catch his name?"

"I was just about to."

"What happened?"

I shrugged. "You showed up. She's pretty torn up about it."

"Love can do that to you. Or even like sometimes. Sorry I blew it."

"She might not have told me anyway. Enough about Rose. Thanks for meeting me. Sorry about the short notice, but Bill's in the shop blowing off some steam."

Hannah nodded. "I heard about the argument he had with Charlie Cobb this evening."

"How did you hear about it so soon?"

"Are you kidding me? It's the talk of the town. I was at the grocery store, and I had three people tell me what happened before I could check out. From the sound of it, they had quite a battle in front of your shop."

"They were both acting like children."

"Men can be good at that sometimes, can't they?"

I nodded. "Bill knows better, but sometimes his temper gets the best of him."

Shelly approached us with an order pad. "What can I get you two gals this evening?"

"Wow, I feel honored being waited on by the owner herself. I must really rate."

"Don't flatter yourself," Shelly said with a smile. "Kelly went home sick an hour ago, and Janie never bothered showing up for her shift tonight. That means you're stuck with me. If you're going to order, I'd suggest doing it soon."

"Two specials," Hannah said quickly. "Is that okay with you, Carolyn?"

I glanced over at the chalkboard where Shelly wrote her daily specials, and saw that she was offering country style steak, mashed potatoes, and cooked apples. "Sounds good."

"That was easy enough. I'll have your coffees in a second."

"I can get them," I said as I started to stand, "seeing how you're shorthanded and all."

"I can manage," she said, "but thanks for the offer."

After Shelly was gone, Hannah said, "The

moon must be full tonight. Everybody in town is acting strangely."

"I don't think it's all that odd both of us ordering the special," I said.

"I'm not talking about us. First there was Nate, and now Rose. Add that to your husband's behavior, and it sounds like the whole town's gone a little bit mad."

"Leave Bill out of it," I said. "He and Charlie have a history of conflict. What was wrong with Nate?"

"I bumped into him on the River Walk on my way over here, and he nearly ran over me. There was a look in his eyes that made me shiver."

"I wonder what's gotten into him now," I said.

"I don't know, but it wouldn't surprise me if we both start howling at the moon like everyone else."

Shelly approached us carrying a tray laden with our food and a carafe of coffee.

"That was fast," I said. "Did you make all of this for somebody else?"

"It's the special," she said as she slid the plates in front of us and filled our coffee cups before setting the carafe on the table. "Why do you think I make a good deal on it? I can do everything before the dinner crowd gets here, and it takes the heat off me. If you need anything, just yell."

I was tempted to scream my thanks but fortunately stifled it before it could escape my lips. What had gotten into me? Was Hannah right? Was the moon affecting us all?

"What?" Hannah asked as I caught her looking at me.

"I didn't say anything," I said as I started to take a bite.

"You didn't have to, I could see it in your eyes."

I finished the apple slice, then said, "I was just thinking about moonlight and madness. They go hand in hand, don't they?"

"You're in an odd frame of mind tonight yourself, aren't you?" Hannah asked.

"No odder than normal," I said. "Speaking of love lives, how's yours?"

She shook her head. "Nonexistent. Next topic," she said, then took another bite.

"What's David up to tonight?"

She glanced at her watch. "He'd better be in class. That's our deal." Hannah's son David had agreed to continue his studies at night if Hannah allowed him to work in my shop during the day. It had been a point of conflict in the past, but hopefully that was behind us all. I hated tension, especially with Hannah. She was my sounding board, my touch stone, and all-around best friend.

I know, it's fashionable to say you should be married to your best friend, but while I loved my husband more dearly than life itself, I couldn't have the honest conversations with him that Hannah and I shared.

"Then I'm sure that's exactly where he is," I said.

As we ate, we discussed a dozen different topics, none of them more serious than Maple Ridge's plans for a Freedom Fest on the Fourth of July. "I still think you should close the shop for the day," Hannah said. "There's going to be fireworks and all kinds of festivities. It won't be any fun if you have to work."

"You know what else wouldn't be any fun? Defaulting on my mortgage. I need all the revenue I can get."

"Things can't be that bad already," she said. "Tourist season is just gearing up."

"Don't get me wrong, we're in good shape. I just want to keep it that way. David doesn't have to work the holiday, though. Did you two have plans?"

"Are you kidding me? Between working for you, going to school, and seeing Annie Gregg, he barely has any time for me at all."

I touched her hand. "You're not jealous, are you?"

She pulled it away. "What? Of course not.

I've come to terms with him having Annie in his life, though for how long, I can't say."

"Are they having trouble?" I'd had a hand in setting Annie and David up, and I felt a little responsible for them.

"No, but she's going to Stanford in less than three months, and I can't see them keeping their relationship going across the country. I just know David's going to be devastated when she leaves."

"He'll get over it, if he has to. He's a grown man, Hannah."

"I don't care if he's forty, I'll always worry about him. You can't tell me you don't think about your sons now that they're grown up and have moved away."

"You're right, of course. But they've gone on to create their own lives, and the best gift I give them is to respect that." Things had suddenly gotten too serious for my taste. "Let's think of brighter things, shall we? How about some cobbler? It's strawberry tonight."

Shelly was known throughout our part of Vermont for her cobblers, and though I usually didn't indulge, I was in that kind of mood.

"I really shouldn't," Hannah said.

"That's what makes it so much fun. We

can split one, if you'd rather do that."

Hannah laughed. "Are you kidding? I don't want to have to fight you for the crust. We might as well get two."

"Now you're talking. Ice cream on top, of course."

"Of course," she said.

"I'll be right back. Shelly's kind of swamped." I went up front, and when I could catch her attention, I said, "Whenever you get a chance, we need two cobblers, with ice cream, too."

"Hang on one second." After she delivered an order to one of the customers sitting at the counter, she came back and quickly fixed our desserts. "There you go. Listen, before you take off, I need to talk to you, okay?"

"Sure thing," I said as I took the bowls. After Hannah and I finished our desserts — worth every calorie, in my opinion — I scooped up the check before she could grab it.

"This is my treat," I said. "And I don't want to hear any complaints."

"I just have one thing to say."

"What is it?" I was prepared for a fight, but I wasn't going to back down. I'd invited Hannah out on short notice for no other reason than I didn't want to eat by myself.

Surely that merited me picking up the check.

"Thank you," she said.

"That's it? No struggle, no fight?"

"Not from me," she said with a smile. "I'll see you for coffee in the morning."

When she saw I wasn't following her out the door, Hannah asked, "Aren't you coming?"

"Shelly wanted to talk to me for a second."

"Good night, then. And, Carolyn? Thanks for calling."

"Thanks for coming," I said.

Shelly was still rushed, but I sat at the counter with a twenty and my bill and waited for her. When she got a second, she took both from me, rang the sale up on the register, then returned with my change. "Sorry, I don't mean to keep ignoring you, but I'm really busy tonight."

"You wanted to talk to me," I reminded her.

"It doesn't matter. It's not that important."

There was a troubled crease to her brow.

After a second, I asked, "Are you sure? I don't mind hanging around."

"I'm sure. Thanks anyway."

How odd. Now Shelly was acting strangely. I decided the best place for me to be was home, and I drove straight there, happily without incident.

Bill was asleep in front of the television, and I wondered how long he'd been there. I was about to wake him when the telephone did it for me. I grabbed it before it could ring a second time.

"Hello?"

"Carolyn, this is Sheriff Hodges. I need you to come down to your shop."

I didn't like the tone in his voice. "What happened? Did someone break in?" I could just see the scattered shards of pottery and broken windows.

"No. Just come down. And bring your husband with you."

"I'm not budging until you tell me what this is about," I said. The sheriff and I weren't on the best of terms, and though I knew I should have cooperated without question, there was something stubborn in me that wouldn't allow it.

"Okay, we'll do this over the phone, then. Just remember, you asked for it. I found a body in the alley out back of your place, and I need you and Bill to come down here."

I felt my fingers loosen their grip on the telephone. A body? Whose? I wanted to know, but I couldn't bring myself to ask.

Beside me, Bill was now completely awake. "Carolyn? What is it? What happened? Is it one of the boys?"

I ignored him and spoke to the sheriff. "Who is it?"

"Wouldn't you rather do this in person?" Hodges asked.

"I need to know right now," I said insistently.

"It's Charlie Cobb, and from the look of things, somebody held his head down in a bucket of mud in back of your place until he drowned in it. That's why I want to see your husband, too. I understand from the talk around town that he had more reason than anyone else to want to see the man dead. Now are you coming down here of your own free will, or do I have to send somebody there to get you?"

"We're coming," I said, a little bit of me dying with the words. Then I turned to Bill and told him what the sheriff had conveyed to me.

CHAPTER 4

"It's not mud. It's called slip," I said as I looked down at the bucket in the alley behind Fire at Will. "It's a mixture of clay and water we use for all sorts of things around the shop, from a type of glue to glazing."

"Whatever you want to call it, it's what killed him," the sheriff said. "How did it get out here?"

I tried not to look at the sheet covering Charlie's body and focused on the slip instead.

"David must have put it out here sometime today," I said, though I couldn't imagine why he would do it.

"I put it out here myself," Bill admitted.

That caught the sheriff's interest. "Why?"

"I was cleaning out the bathroom and saw the bucket on the floor by the pottery wheels. I didn't know it was any good, so I put it back here so I could get rid of it later."

"Was that before or after your fight with Charlie Cobb?" I didn't like the calm accusation lingering in the sheriff's voice.

"Maybe we should get a lawyer," I said to Bill as I touched his shoulder.

"I don't have anything to hide," he said.

"You should listen to your wife," Sheriff Hodges said. "It might not be a bad idea right now to have someone representing you."

"I can answer your questions without advice from anybody else," Bill insisted. He pointed to the slip and said, "I put this out here before we argued. But I didn't kill the man."

Hodges shrugged, then asked, "Bill, where were you this evening?" Turning to me, he added, "I suppose you can vouch for his whereabouts."

I don't know if I would have lied to him to help my husband, but that was certainly my first instinct. Bill spoke up before I could say anything, though. "I was working in the shop at Olive's place. I didn't see anybody, or talk to anyone, either. Are you going to lock me up for that?"

Hodges had been thumbing through what had to be Charlie's wallet, and I saw a thick stack of twenties. "Not just yet," the sheriff said. "That's all. You can both go."

"That's it?" I asked. "You're dismissing us?"

"You answered my questions, at least the ones I have right now. There's no reason for you to be here now that I'm finished with you."

"My husband didn't do it," I said harshly. "You've known him long enough to understand that."

The sheriff shook his head briefly. "I'm not saying he did, but I'm not saying he didn't, either."

"Well, that's a hearty show of support on your part," I said as Bill took my arm.

"Come on, Carolyn, we're getting out of here."

"Just don't go too far," the sheriff said. "I've got a feeling we'll be talking again soon."

"You know where to find me. I'm not going anywhere."

When we were back in Bill's truck, I said, "We need to get you a lawyer right now."

He looked shocked. "You don't actually think I killed him, do you?"

"Don't be ridiculous. Of course I don't. Just because you're innocent doesn't mean you don't need to be protected, though. Who should we call?"

"Let's wait and see what happens next

before we do that," Bill said.

"Aren't you concerned about this at all?"

"Of course I am. I'm not stupid enough to think my innocence is going to save me. But think about it, Carolyn. What's the first thing that's going to cross folks' minds when they find out I've hired an attorney? Go on, say it."

"They're going to think that you're guilty," I admitted. "But who cares what they think?"

He held my gaze. "You do, and so do I. We've lived in Maple Ridge forever, and I'm not about to let everyone in town believe I'm a murderer or that I have something to hide. Okay?"

I nodded. "But if things get any worse, we're hiring counsel," I said.

"How could the situation get any worse?" he asked.

I suspected there were a great many ways things could deteriorate even further, but I didn't have the heart to mention them to him.

The next morning at my coffee klatch with Hannah, Charlie Cobb's murder was clearly the topic of conversation all around us. I hadn't been glanced at so many times, so furtively, since I'd accidentally tucked the back of my skirt into my panty hose at Wilma Birthrite's wedding.

"Can we take these outside?" I asked Hannah.

She took a quick look around, and the gazes of our fellow coffee drinkers swiveled in a dozen different directions. "It is rather like being in the zoo," she said.

"From the wrong side of the bars."

"Let's go find a bench," she agreed.

I looked for Nate so I could say good-bye, but the coffee shop owner was AWOL yet again from his business. I was beginning to think that he'd lost interest in the place — a funny reaction for someone who'd just committed to buying the building.

Outside, it was warming up nicely, a good thing for the seventh day of June. Tourists were already starting to visit Maple Ridge, and my business had picked up dramatically after a long and cold winter. In a few weeks, I'd have to start grabbing my meals when I could, and while I sometimes wished for the lazy days of off-season, I never yearned for the diminished bank deposits they brought with them.

"Carolyn, I've decided to go away," Hannah said, jolting me from the warm glow of good coffee and early sunshine.

"You're leaving? You can't be serious.

What about David?"

"He's nearly a grown man. You've said so yourself. He'll be fine on his own."

"I can't believe you're just dropping this on me." I was losing my best friend in the world, and she was acting as though it were nothing. "When are you going?"

"Friday. I'm sorry it took me so long to tell you. It kept slipping my mind."

"Friday? That's in three days."

She looked at me intently, then said, "You're taking this harder than I thought. Why so glum?"

I wanted to smack her. "You blurt out that you're moving in two days, and you expect me to smile about it?"

I looked over at her and saw that she was doing her best to suppress a laugh. "What's so amusing?"

"I'm not moving. I'm just taking a trip. I'll be back in nine days. I promise."

I nearly wept with relief. "Hannah, for an English professor, your communication skills aren't always first rate."

"I assumed you realized what I was talking about," she said a little stiffly.

"I'm just so glad you're not leaving here for good," I said as I hugged her.

She patted my back a second, then broke

away. "I'm touched you'd miss me so much."

"As aggravating as you can be at times, you have a place in my heart."

"Right back at you," she said.

"So, where are you going?"

"I got a last-minute deal on a European trip. I'm going to Italy."

I took a sip from my coffee. "I'm crazy jealous. I'd love to go with you."

"Actually, one of the other professors on the trip might have to cancel. I'm sure you could take her place on the tour if you'd like to."

I was more tempted than I wanted to admit, but I had just signed a loan agreement for Fire at Will, and my husband had just been questioned as part of a murder investigation. "Sorry, but I can't. There's too much going on here right now."

"Of course. I shouldn't even have mentioned it. How's Bill holding up?"

"He's fine. The poor old fool doesn't have the slightest idea how much trouble he's in." I watched a bird swoop down into the river and come up with a fish in his bill. He looked like some kind of midget, but he was as fast as lightning. I knew several of my friends could have identified him and told me countless other things about his nesting, mating, and migratory habits, but the only birds I could positively identify were robins, cardinals, and jays. The rest of my knowledge about the avian world was pretty much based on size, as in "little bird," "regular bird," and "big bird." It wasn't very scientific, but I didn't need to know the Latin name for a bird to enjoy its song, nor did I have to know the history of every flower to savor its fragrance.

"Are you two going to get a lawyer?" Hannah asked me.

"I want to, but Bill claims it will make folks around town believe that he's guilty, and he won't stand for it."

Hannah sipped her coffee, then said, "He's probably right. You know how Maple Ridge can be."

"What, you mean a warm and loving town that embraces its own?"

"Sarcasm doesn't become you," Hannah said.

"Well, I shouldn't wear horizontal stripes, either, but that doesn't stop me. I'm worried. A great many people heard Bill fighting with Charlie a few hours before he was murdered."

Hannah put her coffee down on the space beside her. "So they're sure it's murder?"

"Somebody held the man's head down in

a bucket of slip, Hannah. It would be hard to claim it was an accident."

I saw her shiver. "I don't even want to think about it."

"Neither do I," I admitted, "but I don't have much choice. As long as Bill's under suspicion, I won't rest until I find out who really killed Charlie Cobb."

"Just be careful." She looked out on the water, then said, "I know it's selfish, but I'd rather David didn't get involved in your investigation this time."

Hannah was dancing on a delicate subject for both of us, and I had to weigh my answer carefully. "David doesn't listen to me nearly as much as you think he does," I said. "I won't recruit him, but if he offers, I'm not turning him down, either. It's his decision, isn't it?"

"The problem is, David doesn't always realize what's in his best interests."

If I sat there much longer, I was going to say something I'd regret. "I've got to go. Thanks for the coffee."

She stood as I did. "Carolyn, don't be that way. I wasn't trying to make you angry."

"You didn't," I lied. "I just have to get to the shop so I can get ready to open."

I didn't even look back at her as I walked down the River Walk toward Fire at Will. I knew how overprotective Hannah could be about her son, but I wasn't about to put him in danger, at least not intentionally. Besides, whether she liked to admit it or not, David had a mind of his own. Ultimately it was his decision. He had a choice in the matter, even if I didn't.

As for me, no matter what it took, I was going to free my husband of suspicion, even if it meant letting the business I'd worked so hard to build suffer, and my friendships, too.

"We were wondering when you were going to get here," Butch Hardcastle said as I walked up to Fire at Will. He was a big, meaty man, with an air of confidence no doubt honed during his former life — at least I hoped it was still former — as a crook. From the word I'd heard on the streets of Maple Ridge, he'd been a pretty good one. He was reformed now, though there were times I suspected he hadn't fully retired from his previous style of livelihood. He was huddled with Jenna Blake and Sandy Crenshaw under the front awning of my shop as it had just started to rain, and I glanced up at the gray-black clouds in the sky and realized we'd probably be in for showers the rest of the day.

As I unlocked the front door, I said facetiously, "I didn't realize we'd scheduled a meeting this morning. Where's Martha?"

"She couldn't get a sitter on such short notice," Sandy explained as we all walked into the pottery shop. "But she'll be along later if she has any luck finding one." Despite her five young children, Martha Knotts somehow found time to join us in our pottery sessions, as well as our investigations.

"Do I even need to ask what this is all about?" I said as I hung my jacket on the peg by the door.

"I thought that would be obvious. We're here to help you clear your husband's name," Jenna said.

Butch added, "Yeah, and don't try to tell us you're not going after the real killer, because we took a vote, and none of us believes for one second that you're going to just let this one go."

I wanted to protest, but it was no use. They were right, after all. "I confess," I said. "You caught me."

Sandy looked shocked. "Carolyn, are you saying that you killed Charlie Cobb?"

Before I could reply, Jenna said, "She's not saying anything of the sort. She's admitting to the investigation, not the crime.

That's right, isn't it?"

I nodded, then said, "I know you don't approve, Jenna, but I don't have much choice, not with Bill's life hanging in the balance."

Jenna took her time answering, then said, "It's not up to me to approve or disapprove of anything you or anyone else does. I'm not a judge anymore. When I took the robe off, I left all that behind me. If there's anything I can do to help you, anything legal, of course, just ask."

"Me, too," Sandy said.

I looked at Butch. "Do you have anything to add?"

He grinned at me. "Just my support. Unconditional support," he added as he looked at Jenna. "I don't mind bending the occasional law now and then if it's for a good cause."

Remarkably, Jenna let that pass.

Sandy asked, "Where do we get started?"

"Can I catch my breath first?" I asked as I grabbed my apron and tied it off in back.

"We're not trying to rush you," Butch said. "We just assumed you'd want to jump all over this."

"Of course I do," I said. "But I've still got a business to run, and I'm just getting into my busiest season. It doesn't make much sense to save Bill and lose everything else, though I'll take that deal if it's the only choice I've got."

"That's why we're here," Jenna said. "Butch and I can give you our full attention, and Sandy and Martha can help, too."

Sandy said, "I've got some vacation time saved up, and if you need me, I'll take it right now."

"I'm touched, honestly I am, but you shouldn't be spending your time off helping me."

"What else am I going to do, stay home and do crossword puzzles? This is a lot more interesting, believe me."

Jenna said, "We know David can run the shop if you need to get away, but we also understand how busy you are right now. So, if you have to stay at Fire at Will, we can do some investigative legwork for you. What do you think of our offer?"

I looked around at my friends' faces and realized just how rich I was. "I don't know what to say."

"A yes will suffice," Jenna said.

"Yes," I said.

Butch grinned. "That's what I can appreciate, a woman of few words."

"Watch it," Sandy said.

"That's good advice," Jenna added.

Butch said, "What say we move on and figure out how we're going to attack this thing? I'll start digging into Charlie's business connections and see if I can turn anything up there."

"He's a building inspector," I said.

"I know that. I'm just wondering if he was putting the squeeze on somebody, and they decided to squeeze back. Inspectors have been known to look the other way on the job, if the price is right."

"Are you speaking from personal experience?" Jenna asked icily.

"I'll plead the fifth on that one, if you don't mind, Your Honor."

Sandy said, "I'll look into his background and see if I can dig up anything that way."

Jenna added, "I'll make a few discreet inquiries as well."

"Good," Butch said. "I'll tell Martha to look into his social life. What are we missing?"

"We need to talk to neighbors, friends, acquaintances — maybe one of them wanted to see him dead," I said. "I can do a little digging there. Just be careful, everyone."

"Take your own advice," Butch said as he squeezed my shoulder. "We can't afford anything happening to you."

After the crew left, I prepared the shop for the day's customers. David came in a few minutes before we were due to open with a sheepish look on his face. "Sorry I'm late."

"Come now, you've got to do better than that. I want details, young man."

"It's nothing all that interesting," he said. "I just overslept. Don't tell Mom, will you? She's been giving me grief about my punctuality lately. She's going to go nuts when she hears I was late for work."

"I won't say anything to her if you won't."

He looked relicved, but I added, "Though I'll have to dock your time card. It's our busiest season, David, and I need you here on time every day."

"I really am sorry. I'll do better."

He looked suitably chastened. "Enough of that then. Help me get things ready for the day."

There were half a dozen people waiting on us when I unlocked the front door and opened for business.

I came back after helping a customer with a purchase and found David dabbling with clay.

"What's that?"

He grinned at me sheepishly. "I was showing someone how to make little clay animals a little bit ago." David loved playing in clay, and it was nice to see that working with it all day hadn't dampened his enthusiasm.

I took the small figurine from his hand and studied it. It was a whimsical little frog figure, and I couldn't wait to see it finished. "How long have you been doing these?"

"It's nothing," he said. "I just make them when I'm bored."

"Well, you should make some for us to sell."

"Are you serious?"

I nodded. "It's just the kind of thing we'd do well with. Can you make anything besides frogs?"

David grinned. "I can make snakes, squirrels, dogs, cats, you name it."

"Then you should."

David started pinching off some clay when I said, "Not now, though. Wait until we don't have any customers."

That didn't happen the rest of the morning. David and I were so busy I barely had time to give the murder investigation a second thought. There was a lull a little after one, at which point David asked, "How did you know we'd be so busy?"

"Would you accept woman's intuition as an answer?"

"You know better than that," he said.

I pointed outside, where the rain was finally letting up. "Bad weather always increases our clientele. Hadn't you noticed?"

"No, not really," he said, "but I guess it makes sense." His stomach growled, and he asked, "Is there any chance I could get a quick lunch before you take yours? I skipped breakfast."

"Go on. I can handle things here until you get back."

"I won't be long," he said as he rushed out the door, still wearing his apron.

I was restocking our inventory shelves in the paint-your-own section when the front door chimed. I'd been hoping the sunshine now peeking through the clouds would bring me a bit of respite, but apparently, it was not to be.

Kendra Williams walked into the shop, a woman less welcome than most in my place of business.

"Kendra, what brings you out on a drizzling day? I thought you had a business to run."

She looked around my empty shop. "Carolyn, I have more customers than you do when I'm closed."

"As much as I appreciate your commentary, I've got work to do. Despite what you see right now, we've been busy all morning."

"Don't you think I realize that?" she said. "I've been keeping an eye on your shop all day."

"That's taking the neighborhood watch a little too far, don't you think? I'm not sure I like you stalking me."

"This is serious. I'm worried about Rose."

I peeked out the window and saw that Rose Colored Glasses was still closed, though she normally opened before any of the rest of us along the River Walk, with the exception of Nate's coffee shop. "Maybe she's sick."

"She's not. When she didn't come in, I closed Hattie's Attic and went by her place. She's not there."

"Kendra, you're overreacting. I'm sure there's a perfectly reasonable explanation for her absence."

She gestured outside, making her muumuu travel in waves I didn't want to surf. "You know how busy it's been today. Rose wouldn't have missed a day of sales like this for anything in the world, and we both know it."

"I don't know what to tell you," I said. "Maybe she just had to get away."

"Exactly," Kendra said triumphantly. "But why?"

"There could be a thousand reasons," I said.

"Name three."

Honestly, this woman was driving me mad. "Maybe she got a little wanderlust and decided to drive down to Boston."

"She hates big cities, and you know it."

"I don't know it, but I'll take your word for it. Okay, how about if she headed into the mountains? She loves nature. If you don't like that reason," I said before Kendra could protest, "she might be visiting a sick aunt, or maybe she just felt like chucking it all and went to the movies. There's certainly enough days I feel like getting away from the shop myself."

"I can see you're not going to take this seriously," Kendra said huffily.

"Until you give me a better reason that I should be, you're absolutely right."

"Somehow I expected better from you, Carolyn."

"Life's full of disappointments, isn't it? Since you're here, you saved me a trip. There's something I want to ask you."

Her eyes narrowed to two slits. "What is it?"

"How well did you know Charlie Cobb?"

91

Kendra shook her head fiercely. "No, ma'am, I won't stand for it, do you hear me? You're not pinning that on me."

"I'm not trying to pin anything on you. I'm just asking how well you knew him."

"He was just another face in the crowd, and that's all you're going to get out of me."

"You seem a little too agitated by such a harmless question. You don't have anything to hide, do you?"

"Carolyn Emerson, every time someone in Maple Ridge gets a cold, you start asking me if I have the sniffles, as if I'm some sort of instrument of doom. I'm tired of it, and I won't stand here and take it from you." Kendra stormed out of my shop, but I wasn't surprised by her behavior. There had been a few murders around town, and for some reason, I always seemed to be in the middle of them. Kendra had connections with the deceased as well, but then most folks in Maple Ridge did. After all, we were living in a small town in New England.

Her rant aside, I wondered if she could be right about Rose. I knew she'd been upset when I'd seen her at Shelly's, but I didn't think she'd harm herself or try to run away from her problems. Rose was no ingénue, and I knew she'd suffered through a few broken hearts along the way. She'd buck

92

up, and if a sudden trip out of town was what it took for her to get back on her feet emotionally, it was no concern of Kendra's, or mine.

I must have still been scowling when David came back from lunch. "Sorry if I took too long," he apologized.

"What?"

"At lunch. I got held up at Shelly's."

"Did something happen?"

"If you call a crush of tourists swooping down on her like vultures something happening, then yeah, something happened. I'd suggest you go somewhere else for lunch." He slapped his forehead. "I didn't even ask if you wanted anything yourself. I could have brought your lunch back to you and saved you a trip. I'm sorry, Carolyn."

I patted his cheek. "That's fine. You've got more important things on your mind than me."

"You'd think so, wouldn't you?" He favored me with that grin of his, and I could see what his girlfriend Annie saw in him. David was sweet, and he could be quite charming when he put his mind to it.

"Call me on my cell phone if you get swamped," I said as I traded my apron for my jacket.

"You won't need that. It's warming

up nicely."

"I'll take it anyway, just in case. See you soon."

He glanced around the empty shop. "Take your time. It looks like we've had our rush for the day."

"If they were only that easy to predict," I said.

I thought about going home for lunch, since I knew Bill was there working on another order, but I decided I wasn't in the mood for company, not even my husband's. I walked over to In the Grounds instead, ordered a sandwich and a soda, then took it outside. Tourists were starting to mill around the walk again, and I couldn't find a free bench. The tourists were a mixed blessing, no doubt about it. One of our previous waterfront tenants had been quick to proclaim that the ideal situation would be for the tourists to send their money to us but not bother to come by themselves. It was that kind of attitude that had driven him out of business in the span of a single season, a modern-day record for Maple Ridge, Vermont. I personally liked the influx of fresh faces, especially after a long winter of memorizing every wrinkle of every single person who lived in town year-round.

I knew Nate kept a few outdoor picnic

tables in the back of In the Grounds for his employees, so I decided to take a chance one of them was free. The location didn't have the view that a brook-side seat did, but there shouldn't be the traffic, either.

Blessedly, both tables were deserted. I sat down and enjoyed my sandwich in solitude, something more desirable at the moment than scenery. David was right: the rain had blown out, and the clouds had given way to a lovely blue sky. The sun was a welcome sight, and I enjoyed the way it warmed me to my bones as I ate.

I was just finishing my sandwich when Nate came out the back door of his shop. The look on his face caught me off guard, and it took me a second to realize that what I saw in his expression was fear. What on earth did he have to be afraid of? Certainly not me.

"Carolyn, I didn't know you were back here," he said, trying now to look calm.

"Sorry to intrude, but I couldn't find a seat out amongst the tourists. Nate, are you all right?"

"I'm fine," he said a little too quickly. "Why do you ask?"

"You look a little on edge," I said. "If you'd like to talk about it, I'm here."

"Nothing to talk about," he said abruptly.

"I've got to go."

Before he managed to get away, I asked, "Nate, how well did you know Charlie Cobb?"

He spun and looked at me. "Why do you want to know that? I didn't know him at all."

"Are you saying he never came into In the Grounds?"

"We get a lot of people here, Carolyn. I can't be expected to remember all of them."

Nate climbed into his battered old Subaru and sped away, nearly spraying me with gravel as he left.

How odd. Was it a rule that the business owners in Maple Ridge had to act oddly today? If so, no one had bothered to give me the memo. No matter. There was a killer on the loose in our small town, and I was sure of only one thing: my husband wasn't who the police should be looking at. But knowing Sheriff Hodges as I did, I had a feeling the only way the real culprit would be brought to justice was if I had a hand in the investigation myself, no matter what anyone else thought about it.

CHAPTER 5

"Carolyn, is your cell phone turned on?" David asked as I came back into the shop. "I've been trying to get you practically since you left for lunch."

"I don't know. Let me check." I pulled it out of my purse and saw that I'd let the battery die again. Desite Bill's constant nagging about keeping the phone charged, I still forgot to do it. "It's dead. Do you know where I put that backup charger?"

"Forget about that," David said. "It's not important right now."

"How can I get any calls if my battery's dead?" I asked as I rooted around in our junk drawer near the register.

"You need to worry about that later," David insisted. "Would you stop digging around in there and listen to me?" Something in his voice told me he was serious, but I was sure he could wait a few seconds.

"Here it is," I said as I pulled the charger

out and closed the drawer. I plugged it in, then docked my phone in the receptacle. "Now, what's so urgent?"

"The sheriff came by looking for you. From the way he acted, he was ticked off about something."

"How could you tell? That's his natural state of being," I said.

"Maybe so, but he said he needed to talk to you the second you got back to the shop. Here's his number."

David held one of the sheriff's business cards out to me, but I didn't take it. "Just put it on the counter. I've talked to him so many times in the past few years I know his number by heart. I'll call him later."

"Carolyn, I don't think he was kidding about this."

I let the sigh forming on my lips escape. "I know I need to talk to him, David, but I just can't face him right now. I will later, I promise." I looked around the empty shop. "Has it been this dead since I left?"

"No, there's been a steady flow of customers. I signed up two coeds from the university for a pottery lesson. There's just one problem."

David wouldn't meet my glance, so I knew something was up. "What is it? What's the catch?"

"They want me to teach them, and not Robert."

Robert Owens, my part-time pottery teacher, was in all honesty turning out to be more trouble than he was worth. Still, he was a gifted craftsman, and despite his occasional rude behavior, the man could teach ceramics from A to Z. I'd be lying if I said his finished work in my display window didn't raise the level of what we had to offer for sale, too. While I wasn't ready to cut him loose, I didn't want to aggravate him to the point of making him leave on his own, either. "I'm not sure that's such a good idea. You know how territorial he is about his teaching."

David scowled. "That's not fair, and you know it. I can teach a beginner class just as well as he can. You should know they both said if Robert was teaching the class, they weren't interested. Come on, Carolyn, give me a chance. We don't have to tell him what I'm doing. It's still your shop, isn't it? This is important to me."

I thought about what it would mean if Robert quit when he found out I'd let David teach one of the classes. Then I realized I could afford to lose him more than I could afford to alienate David. There might be a way out of it yet, though.

"I thought you were signed up for classes this summer yourself. You know the agreement we made with your mother. You can't put the pottery shop before your education."

He looked at me as though he'd expected me to raise that particular objection. "That's the beauty of it. Both girls work as waitresses at night, so this would be in the mornings. Come on, it'll be fun."

"Fun for you."

"Income for you," David countered.

"I won't pay you extra for teaching," I said, reaching for one last straw to discourage him.

"I wouldn't expect you to," he said with a big grin. "What do you say?"

I was all out of objections. "Fine. We'll try it, but if it doesn't work out, I'm reserving the right to pull the plug at any moment."

"Fair enough."

Another thought struck me. "Have you run this past Annie? How's she going to feel about you teaching pottery lessons to co-eds?"

He shrugged. "I'm sure she'll be fine with it. She cleans every day anyway, so it's not like I'll be taking time away from her."

"That's not what I meant," I said.

"Everything's okay," he said, blowing off

my comment. Fine. It was his love life; he could take care of it himself. In the meantime, I had to prepare myself for Robert Owens's wrath. I loved having his work associated with Fire at Will, but his night classes hadn't been the boon I'd hoped for when I'd hired him, probably because he was so reluctant to actually teach many classes. I had enough on my mind without worrying about a pampered potter's feelings.

The front door chimed, and Sheriff Hodges walked in, the usual scowl plastered on his face. David discreetly faded into the back room, and I didn't blame him a bit.

"Where were you?" he asked without any preamble.

"Do you mean when you came by earlier? I was on my lunch break. You were gone when I got back. I figured it must not have been that important, or you would have waited for me."

"I've got better things to do than stand around here wondering if you're even coming back to your own shop."

I matched his scowl with one of my own. "What is it you wanted? Contrary to what you might think, I've got a business to run."

"I need an alibi," he said.

"My husband already told you where he

was," I snapped. "If you want anything else, talk to him."

"I'm not talking about him. I mean you."

I could barely contain my shock. "Do you honestly think I killed Charlie Cobb? Sheriff, don't you think it's time to go ahead and retire? Surely you can get by on a partial pension, and it's pretty obvious your heart's not in it anymore." Everyone in Maple Ridge knew that Sheriff Hodges was hanging on to his job long enough to qualify for full retirement benefits, but to my knowledge, nobody had ever called him on it to his face. Until now.

His expression shut down, and I immediately regretted my choice of words. There was no apologizing or backing down now, though.

His next words stabbed at me like a knife. "Where were you when Cobb died?"

"I was with Hannah Atkins, Rose Nygren, and Shelly Ensign during different parts of the evening. Go talk to them. I know they'll back me up."

He frowned. "You were with all three of them?"

"That's right."

"Was there ever a time after four in the afternoon that you were by yourself?"

I thought about it and realized that there

were some blocks that were unaccounted for. "They weren't shadowing me the entire time," I admitted.

"So your alibi isn't as solid as you'd like me to believe." The man was fishing, and I wasn't about to rise to the bait.

"If I needed an alibi, do you think I would admit that there were gaps? Go away, Sheriff, and don't bother coming back until you have something more than wild guesses about who killed Charlie Cobb."

He stared at me a few seconds, but my return gaze didn't flicker. With a brief nod, he dismissed me, then he walked out of my shop.

David rejoined me in a flash. "Did I hear that right? You should have just thrown a pot at him if you wanted to get him mad at you. It would have had the same effect."

"Maybe, but then I would have lost a perfectly good pot, wouldn't I? If he's going to act like that, he has to expect getting smacked down every now and then."

"Somehow I don't think most folks around here are as willing and ready to take him on as you seem to be."

I shrugged. "Their loss, then. I need help with our bisque order. Do you want to give me a hand?"

He grinned. "After watching that, do you

think there's a chance in the world I'm going to say no to you?"

"That's the smartest thing you've said all day," I said. As we worked up an order, I couldn't help thinking about why the sheriff had really come by Fire at Will. He already knew where I was when the building inspector was murdered. Was he goading me because I'd tweaked him, or had he changed his mind at the last second about what he'd wanted to ask me? Either way, I was sure I hadn't seen the last of Sheriff Hodges, especially when he found out the Firing Squad was running an investigation of its own.

Soon after David and I finished our bisque order, customers started coming back into the shop. I didn't even have to look out the front window to know that it was raining again. Thankfully, at least for the store's bottom line, we were busy until closing. In fact, it was thirty minutes past our regular closing time when David said, "I hate to do this to you, but I've got a class in twenty minutes."

I looked at the clock and was startled to see the time. "Go. I can take care of everyone here. Do me a favor. Lock the door on your way out but flip the sign to "Closed" first, okay?"

"I could hang around a little longer," he said. "Nothing ever happens in the first twenty minutes of this class anyway."

"Your mother would shoot us both. I won't be here long," I said. To reinforce that, I said to the four people still in the shop, "We're closing up, but you've got fifteen minutes to finish your designs."

Then I turned to David and added, "There, are you happy?"

"I guess. I'll see you tomorrow."

"Bye, David."

"Carolyn? Thanks for letting me teach this class. I won't let you down."

I patted his shoulder. "I know you won't. Now get out of here."

He grinned. "I'm already gone."

I finally got everyone out, but I still had a lot of cleaning up to do before I could go home. Some of my customers were meticulous in keeping their work areas clean, and some of them treated my place like one big kindergarten playroom. Today I'd been invaded by preschoolers, if not in actual age, then in general disposition.

By the time I had Fire at Will ready for the next day, I was too tired to do much of anything in the way of cooking dinner. I dialed our home number, expecting Bill to answer, but when the machine kicked in after six rings, I knew he wasn't there. I could let a phone ring off the hook without worrying about answering it, but Bill couldn't bear the suspense. I tried his cell phone, something that was almost always a waste of time, then dialed Olive's shop. Still no response.

Grabbing my car keys, I raced to the Intrigue, got in, then made it home in record time. My husband's truck was in the driveway, which meant he was somewhere around. A quick search of the house showed that he'd been there, but he didn't answer my summons. I was really getting worried now. I hurried out to his shop behind the house, dreading what I might find there. I imagined his body slumped over his table saw or lying at the foot of his planer. What I never dreamed of was how I actually found him.

He was sitting on a chair under the narrow awning out behind the shop drinking a beer.

"There you are," I said. "I was worried sick about you."

"What? Sorry, I wasn't trying to duck you. Grab a beer and I'll get you a chair."

"Stay where you are. You look too comfortable to move." I found another chair, though not a mate, inside the shop and pulled it out beside him. The beer was tempting — I'd had a hard day — but I wasn't willing to take on the calories.

As I settled in beside him, it started to rain again. I loved the sounds of the drops hitting the leaves, and once again I was happy that no one had built behind us in all the years we'd lived here. It was like living in the forest but still just minutes from my shop. I wasn't sure why everybody in the country didn't want to live in Vermont, but I was glad they didn't. There wouldn't be enough room for all of them, and I'd lose my beautiful view.

"Have you been out here long?" I asked.

He glanced at his watch. "About three hours. I just didn't have the heart to work today, you know what I mean? This is a peaceful place to be."

"Especially with no phones around."

He smiled. "I turned off my ringer when I grabbed my first beer. Sorry about that."

"It's fine," I said. After a few moments, I added, "I had an interesting visit this afternoon from the sheriff."

"What did he want, an alibi?" Bill asked off-the-cuff, obviously joking.

"That's exactly what he was after," I said. "How'd you know?"

"I was kidding." The front legs hit the ground. "He's really grasping at straws now, isn't he?"

"At least he's willing to look at somebody besides you," I said.

"Do you honestly think it's any better that he's considering you as a suspect? The man needs to retire and get it over with."

"Funny you should say that. I mentioned that exact same thing to him when he was in my shop this afternoon."

He studied me a second, then said, "Carolyn, please tell me you're kidding."

"I would, but you know how much I hate lying to you."

He shook his head, then killed the last of his beer. "You should know better than that."

"Just because I should doesn't mean I do," I said. "He deserved it, and I won't apologize."

"It wouldn't do you any good if you did," Bill said. "I'm afraid the damage's already been done."

I stood. "I'm tired of talking about this. You haven't eaten yet, have you?"

"This was lunch and dinner," he said as he nudged the six pack of bottles with his foot.

"Come on."

"Where are we going?"

"We're going to get something in you that doesn't include brewer's yeast. How's chicken sound?"

"I could eat a leg or two," he admitted. "But I don't want you to go to the trouble of frying it."

"Don't worry, I'm not going to. I'm too hungry to cook it myself. Let's get a bucket to go, and if you'd like, we can eat it out here. I'm always up for a picnic in the rain."

"No, I've had enough of this view for now. Just make me one promise."

"What's that?"

"Let's not answer the telephone tonight."

I grinned. "I don't have a problem with that, but I don't see how you're going to manage to ignore it ringing."

He shrugged. "Simple. We'll turn the ringer off and let the machine catch our calls."

"What if it's one of the boys calling?" I asked.

"We'll be able to hear any messages they might leave, and if it's important, we'll call them right back. If you're not satisfied with that, then leave your cell phone on. You can answer your calls on that if you want to."

"That would be tough," I replied, "since I just realized that I left it in the charger at the shop."

"At least you'll have a charged battery in the morning," he said. "The world can live without us for one night. Now, let's go get that chicken."

I heard two clicks that evening as the answering machine picked up our calls, but I didn't check the messages right away. Bill and I needed some quiet time together without any outside interruptions. Still, I just couldn't go to bed without listening to those calls, so while Bill was getting ready for bed, I hit the play button on the machine.

The first message was from our son Timothy, just checking in, but the second one was a great deal more urgent: David had been in a car accident, and Hannah was calling from the hospital.

"Where are you going?" Bill asked as I was about to open the front door.

"David Atkins was in a car wreck. I'm going to the hospital to be with Hannah."

"How'd you find out?"

"I checked the machine, okay? I had a feeling in my gut that something had happened, and if you say one word about woman's intuition, I'll feed you hash for a month."

"I wasn't going to say a word. Give me a minute and I'll come with you."

I kissed my husband's cheek, then said, "Thanks for the offer, but I don't know how long I'll be. Go to bed. There's no reason we both need to lose a night's sleep."

He nodded, then said, "Call me when you hear something. I don't care what time of night it is. And, Carolyn? Be careful driving over there. I mean it."

"I'm always careful," I said.

I made record time getting to the hospital, for all the good it did me. It took me ten minutes to get anyone to even acknowledge that David was a patient there, and another five before I tracked down Hannah in one of the many waiting areas.

She hugged me fiercely the second I got within reach. "Carolyn, I'm so glad to see you."

"How is he? What happened?"

"Let's sit down over here," Hannah said as she noticed some other people in the waiting room watching us. Once we were seated near the window, she said, "He's going to be all right. At least it looks that way. They're doing some x-rays, but the doctor told me it was purely precautionary. He's got a scrape on his cheek and he's going to be sore in the morning, but he was really very lucky."

"Did you hear what happened?"

"He hit a deer on his way home from class. It totaled his car, but oddly enough, he saw the deer run into the woods after the collision."

"So it could have been a great deal worse," I said. It seemed like there were fatalities every year from deer-automobile collisions, and it might have been my imagination, but it seemed to be getting worse. Maybe we'd been building too many houses on the land where they lived, forcing them to roam more. I added, "I'm sorry I didn't get here sooner, but I just got your message."

"What's going on with your cell phone? It shot me straight to your voice mail, and your home number didn't pick up, either. Were you hiding from the world?"

"Sort of. Bill had a bad day, so we decided to turn the ringer off. I left my cell phone at the shop by accident, so there really wasn't any good way to get me."

"I shouldn't have bothered you with this," she said reluctantly. "It turned out to be nothing."

"Nonsense," I said as I patted her shoulder. "It surely was something."

A nurse found us and said to Hannah,

"Your son is out of x-ray now, if you'd like to see him."

"Do you want me to wait here?" I asked.

"No, he'll be happy you came. Let's go."

I tried to protest, but she wouldn't hear of it. David was sitting in a wheelchair, clothed in a hospital gown and sporting a large white bandage on his right cheek. When he saw that I was with his mother, he tried to grin, but the bandage wouldn't let his entire face smile.

"Hey, Carolyn."

"Hey yourself. You'd do anything to get out of a shift at work, wouldn't you?"

He shrugged, and I saw him wince from the pain. "You know me, I'm a slacker through and through."

"You're going to be sore tomorrow, kiddo," I said.

"I can do better than that. I'm sore right now."

Hannah brushed some of the hair out of his eyes. "You need to put your ponytail back."

"I would, but I'm not sure I can lift my arms that high."

"Should I get a doctor?" There was absolute panic in Hannah's eyes.

"I'm going to be fine, but my mobility's a little limited at the moment."

She nodded. "Then I'll do it for you." As Hannah pulled David's hair back into a ponytail, I asked, "Where's Annie?"

"She's at Stanford for a few days getting acclimated. She can't wait to move there." The disappointment in his voice was apparent.

"Chin up, David. She's not gone for good."

"Not yet anyway," he said glumly.

Hannah said, "I think we have enough of a get-well committee as it is, don't you? Have they said if they're going to keep you overnight yet?"

"The doctor should be along soon with the verdict," he said as he looked around the room. "What should we do while we're waiting? These magazines are all a hundred years old."

"I can run to the gift shop to see if they have anything more recent," I offered.

"That would be great," David said.

Hannah reached for her purse. "Here, let me give you some money."

"Thanks, but I can manage."

"I insist," she said as she thrust a twenty at me.

I saw David was smiling. He said, "You might as well take it. She won't let up until you do."

"Fine," I said as I grabbed the bill. I had no intention of spending it, but if it made her happy, I'd take it, then slip it back to David in one of his magazines. At the gift-shop I made a few purchases, then walked back to where I'd left them. A young doctor was talking with them earnestly, and I heard David say loudly, "But I'm fine."

I stayed out of earshot until the physician left, then rejoined them. "Here are your magazines."

"Thanks," he said sullenly.

"What happened?"

Hannah said, "They're keeping him here overnight, strictly as a precaution."

"I hate hospitals," David said.

"It's only one night," Hannah said.

I added, "Besides, they've got candy stripers around here. I saw one in the gift shop."

"They're all high school girls," David said.

"I'm not suggesting you start dating one of them, but it has to be better than looking at the two of us."

"No offense, but you've got a point."

I asked Hannah, "Would you like me to go to Admissions with you?"

"No, I'll be fine. Thanks for coming, Carolyn. I can't tell you how much I appreciate it."

She hugged me, and after we broke apart,

115

I said, "You can always call me. You know that."

"If your ringer's on," she said.

"I'll switch it on the second I get home," I promised. "In fact, I'll stop by the pottery shop on my way home and get the cell phone, and I'll keep it by the bed, just in case you need me."

I turned to David. "Get some rest, and I'll come by to see you tomorrow."

"I'll be ready to work a shift in the morning. I'm teaching my first pottery class tomorrow, remember?"

"I've got a feeling you're going to be a little stiff. Why don't we play it by ear? I'll let your students know what happened."

David nodded. "Okay, that's probably for the best. Thanks for coming, boss."

"What can I say? There's no way I could let my employee of the month go to the hospital without visiting."

"It's not that tough a competition, is it, since I'm the only member of your staff," David said with a slight smile.

"So why don't you win more often?" I replied, returning the grin.

I thought about skipping the late-night visit to Fire at Will, but I'd promised Hannah I'd have my cell phone available, and I meant to keep that pledge. At least I could park in front of the shop with impunity, since I didn't have to worry about usurping a parking place from a paying customer. As I got out of my car, I could hear the brook running its course. It was somehow a more peaceful sound at night, and I was sorry I couldn't stop and listen to it more often. At the moment, it earned every nuance of its name, Whispering Brook.

I unlocked the shop, flipped on a few lights, grabbed my phone, then glanced at the store's answering machine. A blinking "1" caught my attention, and I was about to hit the play button when a sharp rap on the front door startled me so much I nearly screamed.

CHAPTER 6

Butch Hardcastle was standing outside peering in through the window.

As I unlocked the door, I said, "I hope you realize that you nearly gave me a heart attack just then."

"Sorry. I saw the lights and wanted to be sure no one was robbing you. What are you doing here so late?"

"David had a car accident," I said. "Don't worry, he's going to be fine. He hit a deer on the way home from school tonight, and Hannah called me from the hospital. They're keeping him overnight for observation, but besides a few cuts and bruises, he's okay."

"That's good news," Butch said. "I've already found out something interesting about Charlie Cobb. Would you like to hear it now, or would you rather wait until morning?"

I was tired after a very long and stressful

day, but Butch was doing this digging for me, and I couldn't bring myself to put him off until morning. "Now's fine."

"Are you sure?"

"Absolutely. I can make a pot of coffee for us, if you'd like."

He shook his head. "No thanks. I can't stay that long. I was heading for a meeting when I saw your light."

I glanced at the clock. "Who exactly are you meeting at eleven o'clock at night? Strike that, I don't really want to know."

Butch smiled. "Easy, Carolyn, it's nothing like that."

I waited for him to explain further, but when he didn't, I asked, "So, what did you find out?"

"Charlie Cobb wasn't all that averse to taking a little money under the table to make his inspections go smoother."

"That's a pretty strong accusation," I said. "What kind of proof do you have?"

He laughed. "Are you expecting me to produce witnesses? The people I talk to aren't exactly looking to turn state's evidence, if you know what I mean. Just know that he wasn't leading all that clean a life. There's a rumor that he took one builder's money, then still failed him on the inspection. The guy was mad enough to kill him on the spot, from what I heard."

That was certainly a motive. "Did you happen to hear who it was?"

Butch got out a small notebook and thumbed through its pages. "Hang on a second. I wrote it down. Jackson Mallory's the guy. Have you ever heard of him?"

My expression gave me away. "So you do know him," Butch said.

"We went to high school together," I replied. "In fact, I was dating him when I met Bill. I can't believe Jackson would bribe Charlie to pass an inspection."

"It's a tough world out there," Butch said. "Sometimes you can't help but cut a few corners. Don't judge the guy too harshly."

"If what you heard was right, he might be a murderer, too."

"There's that," Butch said. "Do me a favor, Carolyn. Don't brace the guy without me, okay?"

I couldn't believe he was suggesting Jackson might do anything to hurt me. "We were high school sweethearts, Butch. I'm safe enough with the man."

"Maybe you were safe with the guy you knew in high school, but people change. He didn't stay in the construction business as long as he has without developing a whole different set of muscles, if you know what I mean. Promise me, Carolyn."

"I won't go looking for him without you," I said, "but I think you're being silly."

"Think what you like, but I'd just feel better if I was around when you corner this guy." He looked around the shop and asked, "Are you about finished up here?"

"I just came by to grab my phone," I said. "Why?"

"I'd feel a lot better if you were on your way home."

I patted him on the cheek. "You're worried about me, aren't you?"

"I don't have that many friends. I can't afford to lose one. Come on."

I turned off the lights and locked up behind us. Butch stood on the sidewalk until I pulled away from the curb, and I offered him a quick wave. Knowing he was looking out for me made me feel good, even though I thought he was off base about Jackson. I hadn't seen Jackson in quite a while, but surely he couldn't have changed that much. At least I hoped not. I had too many fond memories of the man to envision him as a murderer, but based on what Butch had told me, I had to admit it was a possibility.

To my surprise, Bill was waiting up for me

when I got home. "How is he?" he asked before I could get my coat off.

"A little shaken up, but he's going to be fine. You didn't have to stay up."

Bill shrugged as he took a sip from the mug in his hand. "I couldn't sleep. Want some cocoa?"

"What I really want is some sleep. Do you mind?"

"Are you kidding? I'm worn out myself."

He followed me into our bedroom, and as I changed into my nightgown, I asked, "Do you remember Jackson Mallory?"

My husband scowled. "He's kind of hard to forget. I never did like that little weasel."

"Why, because he took me to the prom? Surely you still can't be jealous after all these years."

Bill said glumly, "I'm not jealous. I just never cared for the guy. He always had an angle, even back in school. Why do you ask? Did you run into him at the hospital?"

"No, Butch Hardcastle brought up his name. He said Jackson paid Charlie Cobb under the table to okay one of his projects, and after Charlie took the money, he still shut down the job site. Butch said he heard Jackson was mad enough to kill him."

"It doesn't surprise me," Bill said.

"Which part?"

"Any of it. Like I said, I never did trust him."

I kissed my husband. "Thanks."

"For what?"

"For still carrying a grudge against an old rival," I replied. "Sometimes I forget just how sweet you are."

He shrugged. "I just don't like the man."

I went to sleep smiling. It was nice to know that my husband could still feel a twinge of jealousy even after all the years we'd been together.

The next morning, I packed a lunch before I left for Fire at Will. With David out, I doubted I'd get the chance to eat it, but if I didn't bring my own food, lunch wouldn't even be an option: there was no way I'd be able to get away long enough to buy something. Bill was still sleeping when I walked out the door, one of the advantages of his job over mine. He could set his own hours as long as he got his work done, but I *had* to be at the shop to wait on customers; otherwise I wouldn't be able to make my payments on the building. There wasn't much of a cost difference between my former rent and my mortgage payment, but there was definitely a psychological difference between the two. Hannah had begged off on our morning coffee to stay by David's side, so I was a little out of sorts as I drove straight to Fire at Will without a caffeine jolt to start my day.

To my surprise, Jenna was waiting for me when I got to the shop. "Did you tell me you were coming by first thing?" I asked her as I unlocked the front door.

"No, but I wasn't sure this could wait. I found out something this morning at the courthouse coffee roundup that you need to hear."

"Come on in, then." I flipped on the lights and started gearing up for the day. It was going to be a monster if the shop was busy, and for once I was hoping for blue skies instead of the rainy weather I usually loved so much.

As I put on my apron, I said, "I can listen and work at the same time, if you don't mind."

"I can help you," Jenna said.

"I'll be fine. Have you heard what happened to David?"

She nodded as she took a seat at one of the tables. "Kyle Yates was at the hospital this morning, and he ran into Hannah. David's getting discharged by eleven, and it wouldn't surprise me if he shows up here before noon."

"I don't think Hannah would allow that," I said. "I'm sure I can manage without him for at least one day."

"Of course you will. Now for my news. I'm not sure if you realize it, but there's a group of civil service workers who meet for coffee just about every morning in the basement of the courthouse. I have a standing invitation, but I rarely attend. This morning I thought I'd go by and see if anyone knew anything about Charlie Cobb, since he worked with them."

"What did you find out?"

"Something pretty interesting. Charlie's dad, Jerry, died forty-six days ago. Did you know that?"

"I might have read about it in the paper. He wasn't murdered, too, was he?"

Jenna shook her head. "No, he had a heart attack. The reason his death is important is what the will said. Thelma at the clerk's office told me about its contents, and I thought you should hear the exact way it was worded."

"She didn't reveal something she shouldn't have, did she? I'd hate to think someone was compromising their ethics to help us."

"No, it's public record, if anyone cares enough to dig it out of the files."

"What did it say?" I put down the bisque piece I was holding and gave Jenna my full attention.

"The will stipulated that each of the two heirs had to live forty-five days after the deceased to receive their inheritance, or their share would revert to the other beneficiary. It's quite a coincidence that Charlie lived exactly forty-four days, don't you think?"

"So what happens to his share? I'm assuming Jerry left behind a hefty estate." Jerry Cobb had owned a plant on the outskirts of town, and he must have done well for himself, since he'd lived alone in a five-thousand-square-foot mansion.

"It was in excess of four million dollars," Jenna said. "The interesting thing is that Charlie's brother, Rick, gets it all now."

"What would have happened to the money if Charlie had lived one more day?"

Jenna said, "It would have been a part of Charlie's estate, so his daughter would have gotten it all. As things stand, she'll barely have enough to finish college. At least that's what Thelma said."

"So Rick gets four million instead of the two he had coming to him. Would he kill his brother when he was already getting two million bucks?" The number was unreal to me, a phantom set of digits beyond my scope of comprehension.

"Don't kid yourself. I've known people to kill for ten thousand dollars. Two million puts it entirely into the realm of possibility. We need to look into Rick Cobb's alibi."

"Shouldn't the sheriff do that? I know how you feel about meddling, and I don't want you to go against your beliefs."

"I went to him with the information first," Jenna admitted. "Do you want to know what he told me? The man had the nerve to remind me that I wasn't on the bench anymore and that I should mind my own business and leave the investigation up to him. I've been defending him for years, and he has the unmitigated gall to say that to me. Perhaps you've been right. Sheriff Hodges has outstayed his welcome in office."

"And yet our townsfolk keep reelecting him, don't they?"

"They vote for him out of habit more than anything else. I'm sure of it. If he had one decent deputy, we could run him against the sheriff, but I'm afraid they're all cut from the same cloth."

"The election's five months away, and if you want to find someone to run against him, you've got my support. In the meantime, though, we have to deal with Charlie Cobb's murder. What should we do with the information about his brother?"

"I'm going to look into Rick Cobb's whereabouts on the evening of the murder. That's the first step. I'll keep you informed." She glanced at her watch. "I hate to run out on you, but I have a dentist appointment in three minutes, and if I'm not there on time, they'll chide me as if I were a schoolchild."

"Go. And, Jenna? Thanks for the information. Don't take any chances digging into this, okay?"

"I won't if you promise not to, either," she said with a smile.

After Jenna was gone, I finished preparing for the day, wondering how David was doing. He would certainly be sore from the impact of the collision, but he was young, so I knew he'd bounce back quickly. The older I got, the longer it took me to recover from the aches and pains in my life.

The phone rang two minutes before I was due to open, but since there wasn't a crowd outside my door clamoring to get in, I decided to take the time to answer it.

It was Sandy, the world's greatest reference librarian. "I just have a second," she said after identifying herself. "There's something I'm tracking down, but I'm not sure what I've got yet."

"You don't have to touch base until you uncover something," I said. "I know you have a full-time job, too."

"This might be a factor. I was looking into the open court records on the Internet, and I found something interesting."

"So you know about the will, too," I said, trying not to sound too smug.

"What will? Carolyn, what are you talking about?"

I was confused, but I explained. "Charlie Cobb's dad died a month and a half ago. Charlie was one of two beneficiaries, at least he would have been if he'd made it forty-five days after his dad passed away. Unfortunately, Charlie only made it forty-four."

"I didn't find any of that," Sandy admitted. "That sounds like motive enough for murder. Do you want me to drop what I found and follow up on that?"

"No, Jenna brought the information to my attention, and she's looking into it herself. If you didn't find out about the will, what did you discover?"

"Charlie had a drunk-driving arrest in his past," Sandy said.

"Is it significant?"

"I didn't think so at first, but I started digging into the time he was arrested, going through old newspapers we have here on microfiche, and guess what else happened around that time?"

"I don't have a clue," I admitted.

"Nate Walker's wife was killed. It was a hit-and-run, and they never found the guy who did it."

I couldn't believe it. "So you think he killed Nate's wife, and Nate just realized it after all these years? Don't you think he'd have known about it long before now?"

"Nate crawled into a bottle after his wife died. I doubt he knew much of anything then. Carolyn, what if he stumbled across this information and decided that Charlie killed Winnie? Would he take it to Sheriff Hodges, or would he want revenge himself?"

"I don't know. It's motive enough for murder, if it's true. How do we find out, though? Do we walk up to Nate and ask him if he killed the man? I doubt he'd confess to us."

"Let me keep digging," Sandy said. "I'll let you know if I find out anything else."

"Thanks," I said as the front door chimed. I half expected to see Martha come in with a report of her own, but it was actually a man with his thirteen- or fourteen-year-old daughter. From the expression on her face, she wasn't all that thrilled about being in my shop.

"Listen, I've got to go. I've got a customer."

"I'll touch base later," Sandy said.

"May I help you?" I asked.

"We'd like to paint some pottery," the man said firmly.

The teenage girl sneered at her father. "Correction. *He'd* like to paint some pottery," she said. "I want to go back to bed."

"Sarah, we talked about this. It's after ten o'clock. We don't have that much time left together before you have to go back to your mother's."

"Whatever. I just want this woman to know that I'm here against my will."

My, wasn't she a princess? Putting on my best smile, I asked, "Why don't you give it a try? You might surprise yourself and have fun."

"I doubt that," she said.

"Would you like me to pick out a piece for you to paint, or would you like to find something yourself?"

She rolled her eyes at me, and her father either missed it or, more likely, chose to ignore it. If he could take it, so could I. As a joke, I picked up a bisque clown's face, something I'd made a mistake ordering and wanted to get rid of. It turned out that

131

clowns weren't as universally beloved as I'd once thought, and I still had two faces lingering on my shelves like unwanted guests who refused to leave. "Would you like to do this one?"

"Why not?" she said, barely looking at the face.

I turned to her father and said, "I've got one more, if you'd like to do it together."

It was mean, but I really did want to get rid of those clowns, and he seemed past caring himself. "That's fine."

I set them up at a station, then explained the process. "You apply the paint, I fire the pieces, then you can pick them up in a few days."

The father frowned. "She leaves tomorrow afternoon."

"It's a real shame, isn't it?" Sarah said.

"I'll do a firing tonight, so they'll be ready by lunch tomorrow." One of my kilns was nearly full, so I wasn't pushing it by making the promise.

"Perfect," the man said.

"Stellar," the girl chimed in, sarcasm thick in her voice.

I got out a wide range of colors for them, then busied myself dusting the shelves as they worked. The father chose white, red, yellow, and blue for his clown, while the daughter covered hers from fright wig to chin with black. It was going to be hideous when it was fired, but that was her problem, not mine. She did a few embellishments with other colors from the palettes, but I couldn't get a close enough look to see what she'd done — quite frankly, I wasn't really sure I wanted to anyway. The father put down his brush and said, "That was fun. Sarah, would you like to do something else while we're here?"

"The only thing I want to do is leave."

"Wait for me outside," he snapped, apparently having had enough of her attitude.

She sullenly walked out, and he reached for his wallet as he said, "I want to apologize for my daughter. She hasn't taken the divorce well."

"The teenage years are the toughest," I said. "She'll grow out of it. Just give her some time."

"I'm not sure I have that much time," he said as he overpaid me for the clowns.

"That's too much," I protested, but he wouldn't take his change.

"I figure you earned the rest as a tip. I'll be by tomorrow to pick them up. If I can get her out of bed in time for her flight back to Virginia, that is. Knowing her, she'll be ready at dawn — she's in a hurry to get back to her mother."

"Be patient," I said. "That's what she needs from you right now."

"You sound like you've had experience with teenagers," he said with a sigh.

"I went through it twice with my boys. They do grow out of it."

"I can't tell you how much I hope you're right. It's what I'm living for," he said.

After they were gone, I added the clowns to one of the nearly full kilns and turned it on. Whether they'd ever be back to pick them up was another thing altogether, but I was going to keep my end of the bargain and have them waiting for them. Besides, I was curious to see what the girl had done to her clown face. The kiln would bring it out. That was the thing about firing: the heat intensified whatever it touched, bringing hidden elements to the surface. Sometimes I wished there was a way to do the same to people.

I had a few more customers come in over the course of the morning, and when there was a lull, I decided I could afford to eat my brown-bag lunch outside. There was a bench in view of the shop, just on the other side of the road and next to Whispering Brook where I could get some needed fresh air and perhaps a new perspective on things.

It wasn't quite a picnic — I needed someone else with me to qualify — but it was still wondrous being outdoors. After I finished my sandwich, I tarried on the bench, letting the sun soak in.

The next thing I knew, someone was calling my name. Blast it all, I'd somehow fallen asleep.

Trying not to rub my eyes, I looked up to see David standing over me. "What are you doing here?" I asked as I stood.

"Not taking a nap," he answered with a grin.

"I wasn't sleeping," I said. "I was just enjoying the sunshine. I'm amazed your mother let you out without an escort."

"Or a nurse, either," he answered. "I managed to get her to agree to let me work a few hours, but I can't stay past three. That's when her class is over, and she insists on picking me up."

"You can't exactly drive at the moment, can you? Is there any hope for your car?" David drove an old Mazda that would qualify as a classic if it had been in decent shape.

"No, it's totaled. That's all right; it only cost me five hundred dollars when I bought it two years ago, so I think I got my money's worth. I'll find something else."

"No doubt," I said. "I'm not sure it's a good idea, though."

"I can't very well ride my bicycle around town."

"I'm not talking about that. I mean you coming in today. You should be resting at home."

He took my arm and steered me into the shop. "Now don't you start. It took me forever to convince Mom, and it's too exhausting to go through it again with you. I promise I'll take it easy. You can prop me up behind the cash register if you want."

"It's a deal, but if you get tired, I want you to swear you'll lie down on the couch in back, or I'll drive you home myself. Is it a deal?"

"I guess so," he said.

"I mean it, David."

After a few seconds, he nodded. "All right, just don't pamper me. I get enough of that at home."

Butch, Jenna, and Sandy had given me some solid leads I wanted to follow up on, but there was no way I was going to leave David at the shop by himself. If nothing else, Hannah would skin me alive. I knew I was her best friend in the world, but if she ever thought I'd put her darling son in any kind of peril, she'd come after me like a mother lion. I wouldn't have blamed her, either. I'd do the same if it concerned my two sons, no matter how old they were. Once a mother, always a mother.

We had a quiet afternoon, and I would have been fine handling things by myself, but I enjoyed having David around, and I was sure he preferred being at Fire at Will to staying at home on the couch or in bed.

Promptly at three, Hannah came in. "Are you all right?" she asked David.

"It was touch and go there for a few minutes, but Carolyn wouldn't let me go home, so I managed to grit my teeth and bear it."

Before Hannah could even look at me, I said, "You're not funny, David."

"Come on, I'm a little amusing. Back me up here, Mom."

"I wish I could, but I agree with Carolyn. If you're finished with your little jibes, it's time to go home."

David got up, albeit a little gingerly, and started for the door. "You don't have to pay me for today. I didn't really do anything."

"Nonsense," I said as I patted his shoulder. "If I used that as my yardstick, most days you'd end up owing me money. It was good to have you here today, David."

"I think so, too. I'll see you first thing in

the morning. That is, if my warden approves my work schedule."

"We'll see what kind of night you have," Hannah said. After they left, I started dusting the pieces, a job that never seemed to be finished.

Hannah popped back in, and I said, "I thought you were gone."

"I wanted to get David in the car first." She hugged me, then stepped away. "Thanks, Carolyn."

"For what?"

"Giving David a place to be today, and a sense of purpose. I know I haven't always supported his decision to work for you, but I'm glad he's at Fire at Will."

"So am I, and not just because he's your son. David's more than a creative talent. He's a good guy. I like having him around."

"Well, that's good, because he loves being here. I'll call you later."

"Bye," I said as she left.

The rest of the afternoon dragged on, but it was finally time to lock up for the night. Not that I was going home. Bill was in one of his workaholic moods, and he'd already warned me he'd be busy all evening. That was how he coped with stress, by burying himself in his work. And being in Sheriff Hodges's spotlight was stressful to say the least. I knew that well enough from past experience.

That's why I was going to do my best to clear Bill's name before it was ruined forever in Maple Ridge.

CHAPTER 7

First on my list was my old flame. It had been a while since I'd last chatted with Jackson Mallory, but that didn't mean I didn't know where to find him. Shelly had told me that since his third divorce, Jackson took three meals a day at her café. He was one of the few folks she let run a tab there, mostly because he gave her seven hundred dollars on the first of every month. If he ran short, he made up the difference with the next month's retainer, and if he had a little extra, that was applied to his account as well.

Shelly practically met me at the door when I walked into the café. "You just missed him."

"How did you know I was coming by looking for him?" I asked, honestly confused by her comment.

"You're here trying to find your husband, right?"

"No," I said as I scanned the roomful of

diners. "I'm looking for Jackson Mallory. There he is."

Sally touched my arm lightly. "You're not planning on stoking any old flames, are you?"

"Don't be insane," I said.

"You know the voices in my head don't like it when you say that," she said with a grin.

"In that case, tell them all I'm sorry. I'm not here on a personal errand."

"Well, unless Jackson's taken up pottery, I doubt it's related to business."

I wouldn't have answered anyone else, but Shelly was my second best friend in Maple Ridge. "I'm looking into Charlie Cobb's murder," I said softly.

"Now why am I not surprised?" Shelly asked. She glanced over at Jackson. "I hope he didn't do it."

"You're not sweet on him yourself, are you?" I couldn't picture the two of them together, but stranger matches had been known to happen.

"Please tell me you're kidding," she said. "If he goes to jail, I'll miss his business, not his face."

"I'll try my best not to inconvenience you."

Shelly asked, "Would you like something

to eat? I can bring it to the table."

"No, let's wait. I'm not sure I want to have a meal with him, you know?"

"You didn't feel that way in high school," Shelly said with a grin.

"Fortunately I grew up. You should try it sometime."

"Now what fun would that be? I'll bring you some tea, anyway."

"I'm fine, honestly."

"I don't care if you take a sip of it or just let it sit there so you can sneer at it," she said. "I want a chance to eavesdrop."

"Fine."

I approached Jackson, but it took a pair of polite coughs to get him to look up. He was scowling at first, but a smile broke free when he realized it was me. "Carolyn Emerson, what are you doing here?"

"I thought I'd pop in and see Shelly," I lied.

He looked behind me. "Where's that husband of yours? Wasn't he just here? He doesn't care for me, does he?"

"Bill? He's never said anything to me about it," I said compounding the lie. Trying to smile as I spoke, I asked, "Care for some company?"

He waved a finger in the air. "People will talk," he said.

"Oh, well. It'll give them all something to do." I slid into the bench seat opposite him. "How have you been?" I asked. "How's business?"

"We're doing all right for ourselves. How's your pottery shop?"

"Oh, we're much more than that. We paint ceramics, throw clay on our wheels, and hand-build pieces, too. I bought the building. Did you hear?"

"I might have caught a whisper of it. If you and the other shop owners hadn't exercised your option, I was going to bulldoze your shops down and put in town houses."

It was all I could do not to slap him silly for even thinking about it. Putting on a brave face, I said, "I didn't mean to thwart your plans, but I'm happy with the outcome. We were just starting to remodel when Charlie Cobb shut us down."

"Hmm," Jackson said.

He could do better than that. I said, "You had your share of problems with him, too, didn't you?"

"I don't know if you'd call them problems. We didn't always see eye to eye, but I never had any difficulties with the man himself."

You're a big fat liar, I wanted to say but somehow managed to hold my tongue.

I had a feeling that would be a conversation killer, and I wasn't finished with Jackson Mallory, not by a long shot. "Funny, that's not what folks are saying around town."

That got his attention. "What did you hear?"

"That Charlie held his palm out a lot on his inspection trips, and it wasn't so he could shake hands. I understand the way the construction world works," I said, trying to put Jackson at ease. "Sometimes you have to lubricate the wheels of progress with cash."

"It's been done before, I suppose," he said, "but I never got involved in it."

"Come on, Jackson, you can tell me. I think it's clever, knowing who to grease, and with how much."

He'd loved having his ego stoked in high school, and the years hadn't changed him one bit. "It's not as easy as some folks might think."

"So what would you do if someone double-crossed you? It would make you pretty mad, wouldn't it?"

"Carolyn, is there an accusation hiding in there somewhere?"

I tried to look as innocent as I could, but I'm afraid that particular ship had sailed long ago. "I'm just saying, it would make me mad."

"It's a cost of doing business sometimes," he said. "There's nothing personal about it. If you take things to heart, you're in the wrong profession."

I wasn't about to let him off the hook that easily. "So you weren't mad when Charlie stiffed you and kept your money?"

There wasn't a crack in his façade as he said, "I don't know what you're talking about."

"Oh, don't you?" I decided to try another tack. "By the way, where were you when Charlie was murdered?"

He laughed, but there was no warmth in it. "You're honestly asking me for an alibi? You're kidding, right? I thought your husband was the sheriff's number one suspect."

"He might be right now, but I've got a feeling you're going to pass him on the list, once Hodges finds out what happened between you and Charlie."

Shelly took that moment to approach us with my glass of tea. "Put that in a cup to go, would you? Carolyn's not staying," he said.

"Carolyn is perfectly capable of making up her own mind," I said. "This is fine."

"Then drink it at another table, or better

145

yet, the counter. We're finished here, Carolyn."

I laughed. "Is that what you think? How cute. I'll see you later, Jackson."

Shelly followed me back up front. As she put my tea down, she said, "I've got to hand it to you, you've got guts, my friend."

"Sometimes you have to make a few folks mad to stir things up."

"So, did he do it?"

"I don't know yet. I have a lot more agitating to do before I'm ready to say. Is there any chance I could get a club sandwich? To go?"

"What's wrong, don't you like my company anymore?" she asked.

"Fine, I'll eat here, but I've got more lions to brace tonight before I'm through."

Shelly nodded. "I understand that, but isn't that all the more reason to have a full stomach when you do? I'll have it out to you in no time. You have to have fries with that. A club's just no good without them."

"I'd better not," I said, thinking about my waistline, and my seeming indifference to its expanding size.

"I'll make it a half order. That's barely worth the trouble it takes to eat it."

I felt better after I'd eaten; Shelly had been right about that. Sometime while my back was turned, Jackson had slipped out of the café. I had a feeling I wasn't going to make the cut of his list of best friends in Maple Ridge, but in all honesty, I probably wouldn't have made it before our chat, either. I wasn't ready to turn Jackson over to the sheriff, but the builder had done nothing to dissuade me of the idea that he might have killed Charlie Cobb. I needed to nose around some more before I'd be able to make a definitive judgment.

I wasn't all that eager to go to the next place on my list, but I didn't have much choice. I had to go wherever my suspects were. I didn't normally hang out at bars, not that I thought there was anything wrong with the lifestyle. The world was full of all types, from homebodies to carousers, and if I happened to be in the first camp, it didn't mean I couldn't understand why the second group existed. I was headed to the Thirsty Swan because of its owner, Charlie Cobb's brother, the soon to be wealthy Rick.

It was quiet when I got there, but no doubt that would change as the evening progressed. I knew who Rick was, but it was more because we lived in the same small town than because of our similar social schedules. I wasn't sure he knew who I was, though, and I was hoping to use that to my advantage. A few men glanced my way as I walked in the door, but they quickly lost interest. I suppose I wasn't the dream date they were all hoping for. A short, rail-thin man sat on one end of the bar, nursing what looked like a Coke — what other ingredients the drink might contain were beyond my powers of deduction.

"What can I get you?" Rick asked me as I approached the bar. He was a tall, over-weight man with a crew cut of blond hair.

"A Coke would be nice," I said.

After he packed a glass with ice and added a slight portion of soda from a flexible tap, Rick slid the glass to me. "That'll be three dollars."

I could have bought a six-pack from the grocery store for that, but I couldn't very well balk at the price.

I counted out three singles, then added another to the pile. "One's for you," I said.

He barely glanced at it as he stuffed it in his pocket. I saw a tip jar on one edge of the bar, but evidently the owner didn't share with his employees.

He was starting to walk away when I said, "I heard about your brother. I'm sorry."

He glanced at me, then said, "It was his time. When your number's up, it's up."

"And your father, too," I added. "It must

be hard losing them so close together like that. What was it, forty-four days apart?"

That got me more than a glance. He leaned on the bar and bore down on me. "I didn't know anybody was keeping count. What do you want?"

I should have been ready with a glib answer, but all I could manage was, "Just a cool drink."

He shrugged. "That extra dollar didn't buy you a conversation with me."

"How much would a real answer cost me?" I said, diving into my purse.

He wasn't taking me seriously; I could see that as soon as I looked at him. With a snort, he threw a bar towel over his shoulder and called out to the skinny man at the end of the bar. "Jeff, take my place. I'll be back in a few minutes."

"Should I follow you?" I asked. Maybe he'd changed his mind about talking to me.

"Not unless you want to see what the men's room looks like," he snapped, and a few patrons in the bar laughed at my expense.

This wasn't going well, even I realized that.

I thought about leaving, but not before I drank my three-dollar Coke. At least it wasn't flat, not what I could taste of it.

The substitute bartender Rick had called Jeff came over. "Would you like another one?"

"Not unless they're buy one, get one free," I said.

That got a smile. "Hardly. Rick likes to keep his prices high during the day."

"I could tell from his expression that he wasn't a big fan of happy hour."

"No, the man can be kind of a grump."

I finished my Coke, then asked, "So, what's he doing here? He just lost a brother. Shouldn't he be in mourning or something?"

Jeff frowned. "They weren't all that close. In fact," he added as he lowered his voice, "I honestly believe he was kind of glad. The two of them hated each other from the day Charlie came into the world. Evidently, Rick wasn't all that fond of sharing with his little brother, and that never changed, not until the day Charlie died. Rick gets it all, and he's told a few of us his bar days are over as soon as he can find a buyer for the place."

That was an interesting little tidbit. "Do you happen to know why forty-four was a magic number for him?"

"You mentioned it yourself," Jeff said.

"I heard a friend talking about it," I said backpedaling. "I didn't know what it meant." I wanted to see if the reason for Rick's double inheritance was known among his acquaintances.

Jeff said, "Rick seemed to know, and in the end, I guess that's all that matters. He doesn't exactly open up to us about his personal life."

The owner came back, and Jeff's face shut down the second he saw him.

As he approached the bar, Rick told Jeff, "Back to your seat."

As the substitute bartender did as he was told, Rick turned to me. "Are you still here?"

"No, I left ages ago," I said, adding a smile to try to cut through his sarcasm. It was like trying to use a candle in a hurricane.

"Unless you buy another drink, that's exactly what you'll do."

I stood. It was obvious I wasn't going to get anything else out of him tonight. "I'll be back," I said.

Rick didn't even bother answering, which I thought was a little churlish of him.

Bill was sitting at the kitchen table when I walked into the house. "Where have you been? Do I smell smoke?"

"I was at the Thirsty Swan. The place was hazy with smoke, so it wouldn't surprise me a bit if I reek of it. I'm going to take a shower." I considered burning the clothes I was wearing. It was probably the only way I was going to get the odor out of them. That was nonsense, of course. I'd wash everything later, but for now, I buried them in the bottom of the hamper.

Bill came in while I was still in the shower. "What were you doing in a bar?"

"Paying too much for a drink," I answered as I shampooed my hair.

"If you're going to start drinking, we should probably just get you a bottle so you can drink at home. It's a lot cheaper than buying it by the glass."

"I had a Coke, you nitwit," I said.

"Couldn't you have gotten one of those out of a machine? It would definitely be cheaper than buying one at a bar."

I turned off the water for a second and pulled the shower curtain aside. "Let me get this straight. You have no objection to me hanging out in bars, but if I get thirsty, I should get a drink from the soda machine. Does that about sum it up?" Sometimes I wanted to wring my husband's neck with my bare hands.

"I figured you had your reasons for being there, the owner being Charlie's brother and all. Do you want your towel?" he asked as he offered it to me.

I gestured to the shampoo still in my hair. "Does it look like I'm ready for it?"

"Then put the curtain back. You're getting the floor all wet."

I jerked the curtain toward me, and the blasted thing came down. "I thought you were going to fix that," I said as I reached for the errant bar.

"I thought I did," Bill said as he got to it first and put it back up. "There, it's fine now."

"Until it falls again," I snapped.

"You really shouldn't hang out in bars. They make you testy."

"I wasn't there for the companionship," I said, trying to keep my voice level. "I needed to talk to Rick Cobb."

"Fat lot of good that did you, I bet," Bill said. "The man talks like everybody in the world owes him money. I can't believe you're still digging into Charlie's murder."

"I'm not going to wait around until the sheriff decides to do it," I said as I finished rinsing my hair. I pulled the shower curtain back gingerly, and it managed to hold its grip.

"I don't like it," Bill said.

"I don't, either, but what choice do I have?"

I wrapped up my hair in a towel, and Bill

said, "I've been married to you for nearly thirty years, and I still don't see how you get that blasted towel to stay up on your head like that."

"There has to be some sense of mystery between us, don't you think?" I said. My snit was over, at least for now. I was aggravated with my lack of real progress, not with my husband, and it wasn't fair to take it out on him. Investigations took time, I knew that. I had some good leads now, and I'd chip away at them until something cracked. I dried off with another towel, then slipped into my robe.

"I always liked you in that," Bill said.

"You like me in just about anything," I replied.

"That's true enough. Except for that blue dress you just bought."

Why, oh, why couldn't he learn to stop while he was ahead. "I thought you liked it."

"I could tell you did, so I went along with you."

I raised an eyebrow at him. "What exactly don't you like about it?"

"I'm not saying. I never should have brought it up."

"I agree with you there 100 percent, but you have, and now I want to know why."

He backed out of the bathroom, and I followed him through the hallway into our bedroom. "I can't plead the fifth amendment against self-incrimination, can I?"

"We're not in court, but we might be, if you don't come up with the right answer."

"Any chance you'll buy it if I say you look too good in it, and I don't want other men looking at my wife?"

"Not on your life," I said as I poked a finger to his chest. "Spill."

"It makes your rear end look big," he said softly as he ducked for a blow that wouldn't come.

"I thought it might when I bought it. Bill, it's important you tell me these things before I take off the price tags," I said.

"So I get a free pass in the store when you're trying things on? No consequences, is that it?"

"Within reason," I said.

Bill shook his head. "That's not good enough. If you don't want my opinion, don't drag me shopping with you. If you ask, from now on, I'm going to tell you the truth."

"The same goes for me, then."

He grinned. "That's where you lose. I haven't bought anything new in years."

"That's my point exactly," I said as I saw his grin start to fade. "You need to update your wardrobe."

"Not with this new policy, or from now on, all you're going to hear from me is everything looks fine."

He had me, and we both knew it. "Fine," I said. "Would you like a snack?"

"Do we have any pie?" he asked hopefully.

"That depends."

"On what?"

"Whether you baked one while I was out at the bar," I said.

"Then there's no pie," he replied glumly.

"We can run to the store and get one," I said. I knew how my husband's yens ran, and unless I got some pie into him, he'd be obsessing about it all night.

"No, that's fine. I don't need any."

"There's a huge chasm between want and need," I said as I got dressed. "I won't be long. What kind would you like?"

"Cherry. No, apple. Peach if they've got it. Definitely peach. Or apple."

"Would you like to come with me?" I asked as I finished dressing.

"I will if you want me to," he said reluctantly.

"I wouldn't do that to you. I'll be back in a flash," I said as I grabbed my purse.

"What kind of pie are you going to get?"

"I'll surprise you," I said. I honestly didn't

mind the treat run. Bill's craving had crept into my mind, and a slice of pie might be just what I needed to clear my head and make sense of all of the information I'd been bombarded with lately. It was a lot to ask of a slice of pie, but even if the pie didn't help me sort out the Charlie Cobb case, I'd still enjoy eating a slice, so it was hardly a worst-case scenario.

In ten minutes, I was studying the selection of pies at the grocery store, not sure which way to go. Bill loved apple and peach, and the decision should have been easy, since they were out of peach. I was ready to buy the apple when a lemon meringue caught my eye. I hadn't had one of those in ages, mostly because Bill didn't like them. I stared at it wistfully for a few seconds, then grabbed the apple. I was three steps away when I realized that there was nothing in the world wrong with buying both. So what if I ate too much? I could always start walking to work, and now that our tourist season was in full swing, it wasn't like I was just sitting around waiting for closing time. "I deserve it," I said out loud as I placed the lemon meringue on top of the apple. There would be plenty of pie at the Emerson house tonight.

I was walking toward the checkout when I

happened to glance down the paper goods aisle. A woman was standing midaisle, crying, and helping herself freely to an opened box of tissues. I didn't have to see her face to realize that it was Rose Nygren.

"Rose? Are you all right?" I asked as I approached.

She looked up at me, her cheeks and eyes beet red from her crying jag. I didn't envy her alabaster complexion. It radiated the fact that she was terribly troubled.

"I'm fine," she sniffled through her tears.

"That's nonsense, and we both know it." I put my pies down on an empty section of shelf and put my arms around her. "You can tell me. What's the matter?"

"He's gone," she managed to get out through her tears.

"I know. You already told me you broke up with your boyfriend, remember?" The poor thing was really rattled if she'd forgotten that conversation we'd had at Shelly's.

"No, you don't understand. He's really gone."

I stroked her hair. "I'm sure it feels like the end of the world, but you need to keep things in perspective. It's not like somebody died."

Perhaps it wasn't the most sensitive thing to say, but I hardly expected her reaction.

Rose pulled away from me as though I were on fire, then raced out of the store, leaving the tissue box and its discards in the middle of the aisle. I picked up the half-empty box but decided to leave the rest of the cleanup to regular store personnel.

As I checked out, the girl behind the register noticed the opened tissue box. "We sell whole boxes, too, you know."

"My friend had a bit of a meltdown, and I thought I'd get these for her. By the way, you need a cleanup in aisle five."

I drove home with my pies and the tissues, wondering what had set Rose Nygren off. Then it hit me. I'd said nobody had died, but was that true? Could her secret boyfriend have been Charlie Cobb? I tried to imagine them together, but no matter how hard I tried, I couldn't picture it. That didn't mean it wasn't so, though. Love could do strange things to people. Rose said her boyfriend had dumped her, and the next thing I knew, Charlie Cobb was dead. Could Rose have killed him in a fit of rage? Ordinarily she was pretty mild mannered, but I'd seen her temper poke through her calm exterior before. I still couldn't see her as a murderer, but that didn't eliminate her as a suspect. I was going to have to get someone from the Firing Squad to look into

Rose's love life, no matter how distasteful it might be.

Thinking of my impromptu investigation unit made me wonder if I'd made a mistake facing Rick Cobb myself. The more I thought about it, the more I realized that Butch Hardcastle would have been a much better choice. I'd call him when I got home and have him try talking to the bar owner. I wasn't exactly sure how Butch managed to get information out of people who were generally reluctant to give it, but he had a way about him. In all honesty, I wasn't sure I wanted to know what techniques he used.

I walked into the house and slid both pies across the counter to my husband, but he saw only the meringue. "Carolyn, you know I hate that fluffy whipped stuff."

"Don't get your shorts in a bunch, you little girl, there's an apple pie there, too."

Bill looked startled by the harsh bite of my words. "Hey, I didn't mean anything by it. Thanks for going out."

He looked so hangdog, I couldn't leave it. "I'm sorry I snapped at you. I ran into someone at the grocery store."

"What did Kendra say to you this time? I swear, that woman needs a good swift kick in the seat of the pants."

"She never wears pants, just muumuus,

and she's not the one I ran into. I saw Rose Nygren, and she was having a nervous breakdown in the middle of the paper goods aisle."

"What was wrong with her?"

"Her boyfriend dumped her a few days ago," I said, not sure I wanted to share my theory with Bill until I had more information.

"Isn't she a little long in the tooth to have a boyfriend?" Bill asked as he cut himself a full quarter of the apple pie and slid it onto a dinner plate.

"She's younger than I am," I said stiffly.

"That's my point. You've been married nearly thirty years."

"Some of us are luckier than others. Let me get this straight. Your problem is with the terminology, not the status, right? What should I call him? I can't bring myself to say 'lover,' and 'companion' sounds rather fishy, too, doesn't it? Would you like me to say 'significant other'?"

"I don't know what I meant," he said between bites. The lemon meringue, though it still looked tasty, was dead to me at the moment. The image of Rose and Charlie intertwined was enough to put me off pie for life.

Then I remembered Butch. "I'll be right

back. I have to make a phone call." I gestured to his quickly diminishing section of pie. "You should at least have some milk with that so there's some remote semblance to it being healthy."

"That's a great idea, but not because of nutrition. This thing's full of healthy eating. It's chock full of apples, and everybody knows how good those are for you."

"Sure, without the processed sugar, bleached flour, and thousand and one preservatives."

Bill put a bite-sized portion on his fork and studied it for a second. "I don't care what you say, it looks good to me."

He ate the bite with great gusto, then asked, "While you're up, would you mind pouring me a glass of that milk you were pushing a few seconds ago?"

"You're hopeless, you know that, don't you?" I got his milk, then took the phone and went into the living room. I had to look up Butch's number in the address book I kept in my purse.

He answered on the first ring. "It's about time, Evans. What took you so long?"

"It's Emerson, actually," I said. "Butch, this is Carolyn. Is this a bad time?"

"No, it's fine," he said. "Maybe a busy signal will get the message across that I expect promptness. What can I do for you?"

"It's nothing that can't wait," I said, suddenly regretting the call.

"I know better. I'm listening."

"There's a bar on the outskirts of town called the Thirsty Swan. Do you know it?"

"I've stopped in a time or two, but it's not really my crowd. Why do you ask?" In the background, I heard someone say, "Evans is on the other line. He says it's urgent."

"Tell him I'll talk to him later," Butch said, obviously trying to muffle the phone with his hand.

"This can wait."

"So can he," Butch said. "What about the Swan?"

"I was wondering if you knew the bartender there."

After a moment of silence, Butch said, "He's Cobb's brother. I forgot all about him. Good work, Carolyn."

"Actually, it was Jenna's notion."

"I keep telling her that she's perfect for this kind of stuff, but she won't listen to me," Butch said, his admiration for the retired judge apparent in his tone of voice.

"The problem is, I tried to talk to him about the situation with Charlie, and he brushed me off." I brought Butch up-to-date on the clause in Jerry Cobb's will, and before I could finish, he said, "I'll go talk to him right now. Should I call you when I'm finished, or do you want to wait until tomorrow for an update?"

"You don't have to drop everything for me," I said. "Honestly, it can wait."

"I need to get out of here for a while anyway," Butch said. "I'll touch base with you later."

He hung up before I could protest any further. I wondered who Evans was, and why it was so urgent he get in touch with Butch, but knowing my gruff friend, I'd probably never find out. That was what was wrong with life sometimes: the answers weren't always provided to the questions that were posed.

CHAPTER 8

Bill was struggling to finish the last bite of his pie when I rejoined him, but at least most of his milk was gone.

"You could just throw that last bit away," I said.

He looked at me as if I'd proposed he commit treason. "I was just relishing the last morsel," he said, rather insincerely.

"Go on then, be a mule."

"I don't know what you're talking about." He ate the last bite, then pushed his plate away.

"You're never going to get to sleep tonight on that full stomach," I said.

"I'll suffer through it. You know what? It was worth every last swallow. If I should have trouble sleeping, I'll just remember how good that pie was. Aren't you going to have any?"

The meringue did look good. "Maybe a sliver." I cut a piece a tad bigger than a sliver but smaller than a slice. My husband sneered at it. "That's not worth getting a plate dirty. Go on, Carolyn, have a real piece."

"Unlike some people, I can restrain myself."

"I don't know why you bother," he said as he got up.

After he was gone, I ate the sliver on my plate, then replaced it with another one since I was still hungry and it was especially good. I was just about to start in on it, too, when Bill came back in. "The cable's out again. I swear, every time the wind blows, we lose our signal." He looked at my plate. "Do you mean to tell me you haven't even started that yet? You're hopeless, Carolyn."

I wasn't about to admit that I was on my second piece, though my combined portions were nothing compared to his epic slice. "I'm not in any hurry."

"It's going to go bad if you wait too long," he said.

I took a healthy bite, then asked, "There, are you satisfied?"

"Not really," he replied. "I'm going to go read."

"I'll join you as soon as I finish this," I said.

"I won't hold my breath. Who knows how

long that will be."

I finished my pie, rinsed both our plates and Bill's empty glass, then retrieved the latest book I was reading. I was just getting into it when the phone rang.

Grabbing it before Bill could, I said, "Hello."

"Carolyn, it's Butch. I'm afraid there's a problem."

"Did something happen at the bar?" I could just see Butch in police custody for having questioned Rick Cobb a little too enthusiastically.

"No. He took off this evening. According to the backup bartender, something spooked him."

"What could have made him just run away like that?"

Butch started chuckling, and I asked, "What's so funny?"

"You don't get it, do you? He was probably running because of you."

"What? You can't be serious. I don't think I even managed to get through to him, let alone frighten him."

"I'm sure it wasn't your demeanor that drove him off. I'm guessing it was the questions you were asking. Don't worry, I'll track him down, but it's going to take a little longer than I thought."

"Don't go to too much trouble on my account," I said.

"I won't drop everything — I can't — but I'm not going to let it go, either. I'll ask around, have a few people I know keep an eye out for him."

"Will that do any good?" The United States was a big place, and while I knew Butch's contacts spread throughout the country, I doubted they'd be able to track Cobb simply by keeping an eye out.

"You'd be surprised. Guys like Cobb run to a pattern. I've got a pretty good idea where he'd hole up."

"Thanks, Butch."

"Don't thank me yet. I haven't done anything." He was gone before I could protest. Though I wasn't thrilled with Butch's past, or perhaps even his present, he was an invaluable resource to consult when I ran into difficulties on the grayer side of the law. If anyone could find the wayward bartender, it was Butch Hardcastle. In the meantime, I needed to start digging into Rose's life and see if the man she'd been dating was, as Rose had put it, really gone.

The next morning, I was at In the Grounds half an hour before I was due to meet Hannah. I wanted a word with Nate Walker, and I hoped I could handle it without accusing him of murder. Sandy's timeline connection between Winnie's death and Charlie's DUI arrest could be coincidence, and if it was, I didn't want to be the one to draw it to Nate's attention.

Nate was there, for a nice change of pace. He even looked pleased to see me at In the Grounds.

"Morning, Carolyn. You're in early today. What can I get you?"

"How about five minutes of conversation?"

He looked around the coffee shop. I was glad there weren't that many people there. "I guess so. What's it about?"

"Your wife."

The blood seemed to drain out of his face. "I don't want to talk about Winnie."

"We're friends, Nate. If you answer my questions, I won't have to tell the sheriff what I found out."

For just a second, he looked like he wanted to kill me. Had I pushed him too far? I knew Winnie was the one subject Nate was most sensitive about, but I had to know if he'd made the same connection with Charlie's DUI arrest that Sandy had.

"Come on," he said gruffly. I followed him

through the kitchen and toward the back door.

"Nate, where are you going? Nobody's working the counter," a young woman with flowing brown hair said.

"You take it. I won't be long."

She looked flustered. "I just started. I don't even know how to work the cash register yet. You were supposed to show me this morning, remember?"

"Ashley, I don't have time right now. You'll be fine."

The poor girl looked as though she wanted to cry, but Nate just blew past her. He pointed to the table in back of the restaurant and said, "Sit."

I did as he asked, commanded, really, and realized I'd have to watch my step. Nate seemed to be one nudge from going over the edge, and I didn't know how to keep from supplying that last shove. The outside air was chilly, but it was the frost in Nate's manner more than the temperature that made me wrap my coat closer around my body.

"I'll make this as simple and painless as I can," I said. "Did you know that Charlie Cobb had a DUI on his record?"

"He came in here to sober up after a few of his drinking binges a long time ago, so it doesn't surprise me. Why should I care?"

I took a deep breath, then said, "His arrest was less than a month after Winnie died. Don't tell me you never linked the two events together."

He was crying, but the funny thing about it was, it didn't stop him from carrying on our conversation. It was almost as if the tears had become a steady, reliable thing for him. "No, I never made that connection, but then I was in no condition to notice much of anything after Winnie died."

"I'm sorry this is so painful for you."

"Then why bring it up? What good can come of it now? They're both dead, and nothing I can do will bring Winnie back."

I couldn't believe his reaction. "Still, don't you want to know what really happened to her?"

He stood and grabbed the table in front of me with both hands. The fire in his eyes made me pull away from him. "I've been living my entire life in the past since I lost my wife. It has to stop. There has to be peace somewhere, or I'm lost."

He turned his back on me and walked to his car.

Like an idiot, I followed him. "Nate, you can't run away from this."

"Watch me," he said as he got in and

drove off.

The back door opened, and Ashley, the young woman Nate had promised to train, came out. "Was that a car? Where did Nate go?"

"I have no idea," I answered honestly.

"If he doesn't care about the shop, then I don't, either. I quit."

"That's certainly the dramatic way to handle it, but wouldn't it be better if you went back inside and at least tried?"

"I do need the money," she said, "but I'm not sure I need it this badly."

"Nate's a good guy," I said, despite the way he'd reacted to my statement. "Give him a chance. Do the best you can."

"I guess I should," she said. "Are you coming back in?"

"Not just yet."

I walked around to the front of the coffee shop and decided to wait for Hannah outside. Something kept swirling in my mind as I stood there in the cool morning air. Nate hadn't looked all that surprised when I'd told him about Charlie's arrest for drunk driving. Had he put it together himself earlier? More important, had he extracted his own brand of justice and drowned Charlie Cobb in a bucket of clay slip in back of my shop? If anyone had asked me a month before whether Nate was capable of murder, I would have laughed in their faces. Now, I wasn't sure what I thought.

Someone tapped me on the shoulder, and I looked up to find Hannah standing there. "Sorry, I didn't mean to startle you. Were you lost in thoughts of an endless summer?"

"I wish it were something that easy," I said.

"Let's go in and get some coffee, and you can tell me all about it. I'm dying for a cup."

I thought about steering her somewhere else. The last thing I wanted was to run into Nate again, but judging from the way he'd driven away, I doubted he'd be back anytime soon.

Ashley was at the register when we walked in. "I'm proud of you," I said as she offered to take our orders.

"It's not as bad as I thought it would be," she said. "Kevin gave me a rundown on how to work the register."

I looked at one of the workers in back, a tall, lanky young man with a mop of black hair who was obviously smitten with young Ashley. "Why isn't he running the register himself?"

"Because he's the only one here who knows how to make all of the different drinks. Don't worry, I can do it."

We ordered, and Ashley slowly entered our choices into her register. "That'll be forty-five dollars and thirteen cents."

Hannah said, "Hang on a second. We don't want to buy a round for the house."

"Try again, Ashley," I said softly.

"Oh, dear, I did it again." Without voiding the erroneous amount, she hit a button and the sale cycled through the system. She hit a few more register keys, then with a look of triumph on her face, she said, "Yeah, that was high before, wasn't it? Is ninety-eight cents any better?"

Hannah rolled her eyes and started to say something when I slipped four ones across the counter. "This is what we normally pay," I said in a soft voice.

"Thanks," she said as she put the money in the till. After she told the young man what we wanted, Ashley smiled at me. "Like I said, I really think I'm getting the hang of this."

"You're doing great," I said.

As Hannah and I moved down the line, she asked, "Do you know that girl?"

"Actually, we just met," I said. "Take it easy on her, it's her first day."

"Then I question the wisdom of putting her on the register, don't you?" At least Hannah kept her voice low enough so that

Ashley couldn't hear her.

"It's a long story. Why don't you go sit down and I'll bring our coffees when they're ready."

Kevin brought me our order a minute later, and I said, "You'd better keep an eye on her."

"I am," he said with a grin.

"I don't mean her figure. I'm talking about her math skills. Maybe you should take over the register, too, at least until she gets the basics down."

"Maybe you're right," he said. "I just don't want to hurt her feelings."

"I may be wrong, but I don't think that's going to happen."

I walked over to the table where Hannah sat, and slid her coffee over to her. "There, that wasn't bad, was it?"

"I'm just wondering what kind of brew we're getting, if that register experience is any indication."

"It should be fine," I said, and meant it, too, as long as Ashley hadn't made the coffee. Balancing the report at the end of her shift was going to be a nightmare, but it wasn't going to be mine. Nate deserved it, after taking off the way he had.

Hannah took a sip, then smiled. "You're right. This is wonderful. So tell me, Carolyn, how do you happen to know that unfortunate girl behind the counter? Don't tell me she's a potter."

"I told you, I never laid eyes on her until today," I said.

"My, you make friends fast."

"I was in here before you came," I admitted.

"Couldn't wait to get that first jolt of caffeine? I have days like that myself."

I looked around the room, but nobody was paying particular attention to us. "I didn't come by for the coffee. I had to speak to Nate."

"Well, don't leave me hanging in the air. What did you talk to him about? It must have been serious, if that look on your face is any indication."

"I told him Charlie Cobb may have been the one who killed his wife," I said softly.

Hannah nearly choked on her coffee. "You what? Carolyn, please tell me you're kidding."

"I'm not. Sandy did some digging and came up with a DUI arrest for Charlie about the time Winnie was killed. They never found the driver of that hit-and-run, did they? Think about it. Maple Ridge isn't all that big, and you know how I feel about coincidences."

"They happen in real life, and you know it. How did he react? Why am I even asking? He must have went ballistic when you told him."

"That's the funny thing. I got the feeling he already knew."

Hannah took that in, then said, "So, you think he killed Charlie in a fit of rage and revenge, is that it? Can you honestly see Nate killing him in cold blood like that?"

I took a sip of my coffee. "If you'd asked me that earlier, I wouldn't have believed it, but you didn't see his face when I told him. I was worried about my own safety for a minute there."

"What do you do now?"

"I guess I need to talk to the sheriff," I said. "Whether he likes it or not, he needs to hear about the possible connection between the two men."

"All you have is a veiled reference to the past. It's not much to accuse a man of murder with, is it?"

I finished off my coffee. "Do you think I should keep digging into this before I talk to Hodges?"

She shrugged. "I don't know. We're a little out of my realm of expertise." Hannah paused a second, then added, "Yours, too."

"I know you think I'm being nosy, but the man was murdered in back of my shop, with something of mine. We won't even discuss the fact that the sheriff is sure my husband did it. I can't just let it go."

"I realize that. Just don't let David get involved if you can help it."

We were heading on to that unsure ground, so I had to watch what I said. "How is your son? Will he be at work today?"

Hannah frowned as she finished her coffee. "I tried to convince him that he needed more rest, but he's raring to go. After he finishes his shift, he wants to go car shopping. Can you believe that? If I'd had a wreck like that, it would take me weeks to get behind the wheel again."

"Maybe he wants to get back on the horse that threw him before he loses his nerve."

She nodded. "You're probably right. That car of his wasn't worth much, so we're probably not even going to bother filing a claim with the insurance company. I'll find something good for him around town."

"You should talk to Butch Hardcastle," I said as we both got up from our table and threw our cups away. "He knows how to get some good deals."

"If it's all the same to you, I'd just as soon get something that wasn't stolen," Hannah said. She wasn't Butch's biggest fan, but I was.

"He's a good guy, Hannah. You need to give him the benefit of the doubt."

"Let's just say I'm reserving my judgment." We were outside in front of the coffee shop, and Hannah added, "I'm going to be late. My teaching assistant is going through some kind of personal crisis, and I'm picking up the slack."

"You have a bigger heart than you'd like to admit," I said.

"Don't let that get out at Travers, or I'll never be able to look my fellow professors in the eye."

I strolled to Fire at Will along the River Walk, enjoying the quiet nature of the morning before I'd have to face the inundation of tourists. Our season was definitely in full swing, and I was happy to be busy, for so many reasons. The income would help ease my anxiety about taking the building on as my own, and the distractions offered by vacationing families painting pottery would fill my days. I'd still find time to do a little digging, but even if I didn't, I had the Firing Squad working on Charlie Cobb's murder for me.

Apparently more than I realized.

Martha Knotts was waiting for me when I

got to Fire at Will. She was a petite young woman with sparkling eyes, and every time I saw her, I was amazed that she had five children at home.

I smiled at her as I unlocked the door. "Good morning. You're out awfully early, aren't you?"

"I had an aerobics class this morning, and my dear husband agreed to stay with the kids until I get back." She grinned impishly. "Now I'm shamelessly taking advantage of him."

"Good for you," I said. "Would you like to come in?"

"No, I'd really better get back home. I just wanted to tell you something I heard in class today."

I knew Martha had the best connections and networking web across town with her activities schedule. Between the children and her own varied interests, Martha was a one-woman grapevine. "Go on, I'm listening."

She glanced toward Rose Colored Glasses. "Rose Nygren just lost a boyfriend, and she's been taking it pretty hard."

"I know. She's been crying on my shoulder."

Martha looked a little disappointed that I'd already heard the news. "Did you know who she was dating?"

"No, I haven't been able to get that out of her yet," I admitted. "Why, do you know?"

"That's what makes it so interesting. My source wasn't sure, but she had it narrowed down to one of two men. Charlie Cobb made the short list," she said triumphantly.

That confirmed my own recent suspicions. "So that implies that she might have had something to do with what happened to him," I said.

"Maybe, but there's something else. Do you want to know who the other candidate is?"

"You've certainly got my attention."

Martha smiled slightly. "His brother, Rick. He owns the Thirsty Swan."

"We've met," I said.

Martha added, "My friend says there's another twist to this, but I'm not sure if it's true."

"When has that ever stopped us from talking about it before?" I asked. "Sometimes we have to sort through the fantasy to get to the fact."

Martha nodded. "For what it's worth, my friend seems to think that Rose may have been dating them both at the same time. When the brothers found out what she was up to, they both dumped her. I thought it was motive enough for murder, either for Rose or Rick, so I came straight to you."

"Thanks. Let me see what I can uncover," I said.

"Keep me in the loop, okay? Inquiring minds and all that," Martha said, smiling as she left.

As I got ready to open the shop for business, I thought about what Martha had told me. Could Rose Nygren really have been dating two men at the same time? Anything was possible. The older I got, the more I realized that. In matters of the heart, we never seemed to gain much wisdom, and there weren't many actions more foolhardy than dating brothers in such a small town and trying to keep it a secret.

But at this point, it was just a rumor, and I was going to treat it as such until I found proof one way or the other. Still, if it were true, would it have been enough to lead her to murder? And if so, why did she kill Charlie, especially when his brother, Rick, was such a nastier customer? I was still puttering around the shop, not getting much of anything done, when David walked in.

"Good morning," he said. The bandage on his cheek was smaller today, further proof that he was starting to heal.

"Morning," I replied. I glanced out the

window and saw Rose opening her shop. "I'll be right back."

"I'm fine, thank you. And you?"

I looked at David and saw him smiling. "Sorry, I'm a little distracted. How are you feeling today?"

He flexed his arms. "The stiffness is almost gone. I'm ready to tackle the world again." His fingers gingerly touched the bandage on his face. "I was able to change this down to a manageable size, too."

"If I'd been in your shoes, I would have stayed in bed for a month," I said.

"I don't believe it for a second," he said.

"It's true. Anyway, I've got everything ready to open, and I should be back before then."

David nodded. "Take your time. After all, you are the boss."

"That's right, I am, aren't I? I'll be at Rose's if you need me."

He mounted the stool behind the register and said, "I'll be fine. My class is today, don't forget."

"You're taking something at the college in the daytime?" I asked. That would put a serious cramp in my style, but I couldn't begrudge him his education.

"No, I'm talking about my pottery lessons. You gave me your permission, remember?"

"Of course I do, I'm not daft. I just figured you'd cancel or at least postpone them."

"Why in the world would I want to do that?"

"You were just in an accident, David. Is it a good idea for you to teach right now?"

He shook his head. "You're as bad as —"

"Don't say it," I warned him.

"I won't, but you are. Besides, how much heavy lifting am I going to have to do? I believe in low-impact pottery."

"I'm sure you do. It's your students I'm not so sure about. Don't worry, I'll be back in plenty of time for you to teach your star pupils."

I doubted the coeds who'd signed up were all that interested in pottery. If David had been teaching rug hooking or scuba diving, they would have been first in line for lessons as well. Not that it should matter to me. The classes would add a little income to our bottom line, and that was never a bad thing.

I left him, still smiling, and I walked over to Rose's. It was time the two of us had a talk.

I had to get by Kendra's gauntlet first, though. The woman was out in front of the shop waiting to swoop down on the next passerby, and before I could scurry past her shop, she got her hooks into me.

CHAPTER 9

"Carolyn Emerson, don't you ever call me a busybody again, do you hear me?"

"Kendra, when have I ever called you that before?" I asked. I hadn't, either, at least not to her face.

"The implication's been there, and there's no use trying to deny it."

"Then I won't. So, why do I have to stop?"

"Because you're a thousand times worse than I am, and you know it. I've heard you've been digging into every mystery that's happened in Maple Ridge in the past twenty years."

I tried my best to look innocent. "If that's true, which I'm not admitting for a second, how did you find out about it? Have you been doing some snooping on your own?"

She managed to look offended, but I was willing to bet a month's income at my shop against her closet full of muumuus that I was right. "Can I help it if people choose to unload their spiritual woes and burdens onto me? Would you have me turn them away?"

"I really don't have time for this," I said as I tried to brush past her. "I need to talk to Rose."

"She's what I'm talking about. You're just dying to know who she was dating, aren't you?"

"Come on, Kendra, you need to keep up with the times. That's yesterday's news." Though, I'd received the information less than an hour earlier, I figured a little embellishment never hurt now and then.

She didn't even try to hide her disappointment. "Where exactly did you hear about that? I sincerely doubt Rose told you."

"For that matter, I'm willing to bet she didn't confide in you, either," I said.

Kendra shrugged. "I can't help but hear things around town. You should be careful. Nate has a nastier bite than you might think."

"Now how on earth did you hear about that?" The woman was absolutely amazing.

She looked at me smugly as she said, "You were overheard. Do you honestly think that Charlie Cobb was the only one in town who ever drank and drove back when Winnie was run down?"

How on earth had she learned the gist of my conversation with Nate so soon after it had happened? The only thing I could think of was that she had a spy at In the Grounds. She had to. I promised myself to watch what I said around the place until I found her connection. She'd raised an intriguing point, though.

"Who else could have done it?" I asked.

"Think about one thing, Carolyn. Nate has held on to the memory of his wife for an extraordinarily long time, don't you think?"

"He loved her," I said. "What's wrong with that?"

"Nothing. I happen to believe that, too, no matter what my personal track record might indicate. But other people suffer tragic losses, and they manage to move on with their lives. Not Nate, though."

"If there's one thing I've learned over the years," I said, "it's that everybody is different, and they react to tragedies in different ways."

"That's true, but have you ever stopped to think that Nate might be feeling more than his loss? How about a measure of guilt thrown in?"

"Are you saying that you believe Nate killed his own wife?" The idea was so far beyond any scope of rational thought, I couldn't accept it.

"Not necessarily, but he was a heavy drinker back then, and after he crawled out of the bottle, he never had another drink as far as I know."

"Still, I can't see him doing it," I said.

"It's a possibility our sheriff considered for a while, I know that. You should ask him about it."

"He doesn't exactly take me into his confidence these days," I said. "Why should he talk to me about what he thinks?"

"Because he hates the fact that he never solved the case. There's something you don't know about John Hodges. He wants to retire with all of the major cases on his desk solved, and Winnie Walker's death is a nagging loose thread he wants to tie off. You might just be surprised to find out he's an ally."

"Why do you care?" I asked Kendra point-blank. "Forgive me for saying so, but you've never shown all that much interest in help-ing me in the past."

"Take it for what it's worth," she said. "I just thought you should know that not everything is as it seems."

Kendra ducked back into her shop, and I made my way to Rose's. Could the woman be right about Nate and his wife? Was his obsession with Winnie simply a distraught husband's anguish, or was there a healthy dose of guilt thrown in? Either way, I was going to have to focus more of my resources on Nate Walker's life, both past and present.

But before I could do that, I needed to talk to Rose. She was still a viable suspect on my list, no matter what Kendra had told me. Then it struck me. Was that why Kendra had been so forthright about Nate? Was she doing it to muddy the waters to try to protect Rose? And if that was true, why did Rose need protection from anybody, especially me? The more I learned about my fellow townsfolk in Maple Ridge, the more I wondered exactly how well I really knew my friends and neighbors.

"Hi, Rose," I said as I neared her shop. She was setting up a display of sun catchers that managed to catch the slightest breath of wind. Many times when I looked out my window, I saw them dancing in the breeze. It was a great way to capture attention for her shop.

"Hello, Carolyn. I wish I had time to chat, but I'm in a bit of a hurry."

"This won't take long. You wouldn't believe the stories I've been hearing about you around town. I thought you should know, before any of them got back to you."

"I don't think I could care less about what anyone might have to say about me," she said.

"It's not at all flattering. I could defend you better if I knew what the truth was. Were you dating Charlie and Rick Cobb at the same time?"

Rose's stunned expression left me no doubt that she was innocent, at least of double-dating a pair of brothers.

"I never went out with Charlie Cobb in my life," Rose said firmly, and I believed her. "And now that Rick has dumped me, I'm through with men forever."

On the last point I wasn't convinced. I knew Rose had given up on men at least half a dozen times in her life so far. "Why did he break up with you, then?"

She whimpered a little, then said, "I don't want to talk about it."

"I'm a good listener, or so I've been told," I said.

Rose looked up and down the street, and perhaps I imagined it, but her gaze seemd to linger in Kendra's direction a little longer than it did anywhere else. "It was about money," she said.

That wasn't what I was expecting. "Did he want yours?"

She shook her head. "No, that was the problem. The second he found out Charlie was dead, Rick brushed me off. He said now that he was loaded, he could do a whole lot better than me." That brought on a full torrent of tears, and I wished I'd waited to confront her until we'd gotten inside her shop. I maneuvered her inside, then closed the door behind us. As I hugged her, Rose let it out, shaking me with her sobs. "What's wrong with me, Carolyn? Why can't I keep a boyfriend?"

I wasn't about to venture into those uncharted waters. "Honey, it's not you. The world is full of idiots. You just seem to catch more than your share of them."

"You're right; all men are pigs."

I pulled away from her. "Wait a second, that's not true. I know for a fact that there are good men out there. I married one myself."

She dabbed at her cheeks. "You've been married thirty years. How do you know there are any good ones left?"

"I see them all the time, and you would, too, if you weren't so busy going out with the wrong guys." It was blunt talk, but she'd asked me, and I wasn't about to tiptoe around it.

"How can you tell the good ones from the

bad ones?" she asked.

"Listen to your head, as well as your heart."

"That advice is too general to do me any good," Rose said. "I need more than that."

"Okay, for a starter, ask yourself some questions. Is he polite? Does he listen to your answer when he asks you a question, or is he just waiting for his turn to talk? Is he nice to people he doesn't have to be nice to? How does he treat his mother? Is he willing to pick up the check every now and then? Things like that."

"I guess that helps a little," she said reluctantly.

"Well, that's all I have time for," I said. "You could always ask someone else for advice."

Rose frowned. "Not Kendra. She doesn't want me to date anyone. She thinks I'm too good for them all."

"That's dangerous advice to heed," I said. "Leave yourself open to new experiences. Go places you wouldn't ordinarily go. Take a different way home. Find a new hobby. I know Maple Ridge isn't all that big a town, but we're in the heart of our tourist season. There must be a thousand ways to put yourself out there. Oh, and one more thing."

"What's that?"

"Stay away from married men. Especially mine," I added with a grin.

She tried to return the smile, but she managed only a small, crooked grin. How on earth had I gotten myself into this conversation? It was my own fault, asking her about her love life, but how else would I have known if the rumors I'd been hearing were true? A question lingered in my mind. Why did Rick wait until Charlie was dead to dump Rose? Was there really that big a difference between inheriting four million dollars and inheriting two? Or had he just used that as an excuse to sever their relationship? And more important, how was I going to find out? I wondered if Butch had had any luck tracking down Rick. If he hadn't, I had a few more questions to add to the list.

I escaped Rose's grasp as quickly as I could and hurried back to Fire at Will. At least Kendra was now inside, so I didn't have to physically duck out of her way as I passed her shop.

David was chatting with two coeds inside, and I realized they were there for their inaugural pottery lesson.

"Good, you're here," he said when he saw me. "We can get started with our class now."

"Just leave the door open," I said with a smile.

"There's no door between the paint stations and the pottery," David said.

One of the coeds looked just as baffled as David did, but the other one grinned instantly. "We'll be good. I promise."

"You'd better. He has a girlfriend."

David said, "She's at Stanford."

"But she's coming back," I added.

As he started their lesson on basic throwing techniques, I tried not to eavesdrop, but it was hard not to listen to David's sincere patter as he demonstrated how to knead the clay and slam it onto the wheel. I peeked around the corner and saw that one of the coeds seemed to be interested in the lesson. The other? All she was interested in was David. Funny thing, though. The one focused on my assistant was not the one I'd traded quips with. It was going to be an interesting session.

I was just sorry I didn't get to hear any more of it. A pair of women in their midtwenties came in dressed in Prada dresses and Manolo Blahnik shoes. "We're bored," the frosted blonde said.

"Entertain us," her redheaded companion said.

"If you're looking for the dancing monkey, she's next door."

The blonde curled her upper lip. "There's

actually a monkey there? How gross."

"Is it a good dancer, or does it just shift from foot to foot? Or is it paw? What do you call a monkey's foot?"

"Why don't you go ask the woman with the monkey?" I said. I could just imagine them approaching Kendra at Hattie's Attic, demanding to see a dancing monkey she'd never heard of. I was in the crafting business, and while I hoped my customers were entertained by what they did at Fire at Will, I wasn't exactly a stand up comic.

"Enough talk about the monkey," the redhead said. She pointed to one of David's surrealist teapots in the display window. "I want to make one of those. Teach me."

"Would you like to build one from raw clay, or would you rather just paint one?" Maybe I'd get some extra income from the pair.

"After we decorate them, can we just take them home?" the blonde asked me.

"No, they have to be fired in the kiln. You can pick them up in a few days."

She shook her head. "We don't have days to wait."

"Are you leaving tomorrow?" I asked. I could do a priority firing if I had to, but I was going to charge them for the privilege.

"No, we're stuck here for the next four

days while our husbands attend some kind of corporate retreat."

"Then they'll be ready for you before you go. I promise."

The blonde looked at the redhead, and they both shook their empty little heads in near perfect unison. "We don't want to wait."

"Well then, your only option is to buy one already made."

The redhead looked toward the window. "But there's just one of them on display."

The blonde said, "I'm sure she has a dozen more in back."

"Ladies, these items are one-of-a-kind handmade pieces of art. They don't come off a production line, and you won't see a duplicate in any of your friends' kitchens."

"I want it," the blonde said suddenly.

"It's mine," the redhead retorted. "I saw it first."

The blonde lunged for it, and the redhead hit her hand, shattering the teapot on the floor.

"Now look what you've done," the blonde said accusingly.

"You dropped it," the redhead said.

I moved between them and the front door. "I don't care who pays for it, but one of you is going to cough up the money."

"It was an accident," the blonde said. "That makes it nobody's fault."

"You've got insurance. Let them cover your losses," the redhead said.

I didn't budge. "Ladies, there's a deputy sheriff in the other room, and all I have to do is raise my voice and he'll come out here. He's a pottery buff, and he visits here on his day off."

"You're bluffing," the blonde said. "There's nobody back there."

I raised my voice and said, "David, could you come here a second?"

My assistant popped his head around the corner. "Is something wrong?"

"I was just telling these young ladies about —"

"Nothing. We don't need you. We're fine," the redhead said.

"Absolutely fine," the blonde agreed. "We've got it covered."

"Carolyn?" David asked.

"Go back to what you were doing."

He looked puzzled by the summons, but David quickly disappeared again.

"You didn't have to call him out here," the blonde said in an accusatory tone of voice.

"We were going to pay you," the redhead said.

I was tired of them both. "Then I suggest you do so."

I inflated the price, which they paid without batting their heavily done eyelashes. It wasn't out of spite or meanness. Okay, maybe a little, but the main reason was because I'd loved that teapot, and I'd wanted it to go to a good home, not to end up shattered into shards on the floor of the shop. They each handed me a credit card, ordering me to split the bill in half, and they were still grumbling as they left a few minutes later. As I swept up the pieces, I put the usable sections aside for a mosaic and discarded the rest.

A little later, David came out with his students and said to me, "Carolyn, could you ring up two lessons? They're coming back in a few days for the next session, but I told them unless we made other arrangements, it's a pay-as-you-go proposition."

I took the girls' fees, and David walked them out the door.

When he came back in, I asked, "How was class?"

"Suzy did a good job, but Helen kept asking me the most inane questions. I was ready to scream."

"You didn't, though, because I would have heard you. What did you think of my customers?"

He shrugged. "I wasn't exactly sure why you called me out here. You weren't trying to fix me up with one of them, were you?"

I laughed at the suggestion. David misinterpreted it. "Come on. Be nice. I'm not that hideous, am I?"

"David, my friend, neither one of those women were worthy of you. Trust me on that."

"So why the summons?"

"I told them you were a deputy in town," I admitted.

"You what? Why on earth would you do that?"

I pointed to the shattered teapot pieces. "They broke your pot, and then they tried to duck out without paying. You're not too upset, are you?"

He shook his head as he looked at the ruined work. "I'm kind of glad they did it."

"Why would you say something like that?" Sometimes my assistant surprised me. Out of the reactions I'd been expecting, gratitude was not even on the list.

"The handle was out of line, and the spout had a twist in it that I never could get right."

"I thought it was a beautiful piece," I said.

"You're prejudiced though, aren't you? How much did you charge them?"

When I told him, his jaw dropped. "I should get a raise, if that's what you're getting for my work."

I went to the cash register and pulled out a twenty. "Don't let it go to your head, but here's a bonus for you. I clipped them at a pretty good rate myself."

He took the twenty without protest and folded it before he stuck in his front pocket. "Carolyn, do you make a habit of gouging people?"

"Just if they annoy me," I said. "Think of that as a tip."

"But you didn't get one," he protested.

"Don't worry, I made a little for myself, too. Why don't you get busy and make a replacement for the teapot they broke? And watch that twist, would you?"

I was teasing, but he didn't catch it. "I'll get it right this time."

Fascinated, I watched David as he quickly hand-built the basic teapot shape out of rolled sheets of clay. In no time at all, he had the basic frame, with a sealed bottom and a lid for the top. "I thought you usually turned the lids for your teapots on the wheel out of the clay left over after you finish turning the pot," I said.

"I do, but I've been experimenting lately, and I like the look I get this way."

"It's still fun to watch you turn a pot and then make the top out of the same matching piece of clay."

"Yeah, but I can get some pretty extraordinary shapes building them by hand." He studied his box shape, then said, "I'll do the handle and the spout as soon as this gets leather hard. That's when I'll add the embellishments, too."

"Why don't you make a few more while you're at it?"

"Carolyn, I don't do production work, and you know it."

I looked at our inventory. "Somebody's got to, and if you won't, I'll have to get Robert Owens back in here."

"Okay, fine, I'll do it," David said as he started wedging another block of clay.

"I'll do some cleaning while you do that," I said.

"You can make some pots, too, you know."

"What, and deprive you of all the fun? No, I'll make something later."

It was twenty minutes before David's lunch break when the front door opened. Butch Hardcastle came in with a broad grin on his face. "Is David here?"

"He's working in back," I said. "Why? What's going on?"

"Come out here a second," he said.

I followed him out, wondering what could make Butch smile like that. He pointed to a shiny red Triumph TR3. "What do you think?"

"It's pretty, but how in the world do you get in and out of it? You must need a shoehorn and a tub of bacon grease."

"It was a tight fit coming over," Butch admitted, "but it's not for me. I picked it up for David."

I looked at the car, then looked at Butch. "You know he can't afford anything that nice."

"That's the thing. I got it in a sweet deal, and I thought it would be perfect for him. I can make his payments so tiny he won't even notice them."

I could just imagine how Hannah would react to that suggestion, but I had to be careful about what I said to Butch. "I don't know how to put this, but is it on the up-and-up?"

"Carolyn Emerson, do you think for one second I would bring your assistant a hot car? This one's not even warm to the touch," he said as he stroked the rear fender.

"Then how did you get it? Wait a second, that didn't come out right. How can you afford to give it to David so inexpensively? There, that's better."

Butch shrugged. "A friend of a friend of a friend owed me a favor, and this is how he paid it back. It's in good shape, and the second I saw it, I thought of David. He still needs transportation, doesn't he?"

There was a loophole in that question, and I decided to exploit it if I could. "That's the thing. I think Hannah already took care of it."

Butch looked at the Triumph. "It can't be as sweet as this, can it?"

"I sincerely doubt that," I said. "Should we ask her and see what she says?"

"Maybe it wasn't that great an idea after all," Butch said, obviously crestfallen. "Hannah's not exactly my biggest fan."

"She's just cautious sometimes," I said as I gave Butch a peck on the cheek.

"Hey, what was that for?" he asked as he looked around the street for anyone watching us.

"It was a sweet thought, and I'm sure David would have appreciated it."

"If he ever heard about the offer, you mean," Butch said, adding a slight smile to take some of the sting out of his words. "Maybe we should just forget about the whole thing."

"It was a wonderful gesture," I assured him.

Butch shrugged. "I've got an idea. I could always park that boat I've been driving and shoot around town in this thing myself."

"I bet it looks good on you," I said.

He managed to squeeze his large frame into the front seat, but I didn't know how he was going to steer it with the wheel shoved into his chest.

David joined me on the sidewalk as I watched Butch drive away. "Was that Butch Hardcastle?" he asked me.

"It was. What do you think of his car?"

David scratched his chin. "I know it probably sounds crazy, but I've never been a big fan of convertibles. How's he going to get out of it?"

"I don't know, but I hope he's not in any hurry when he gets wherever he's going. How's your mother doing on your car search?"

David frowned. "My aunt Patty's got a Volvo she was getting ready to trade in, so Mom's paying her the value of it for me. There's a car for picking up the ladies."

"I don't think Annie will mind when she gets back into town," I said.

"If she comes back," David said glumly. "I talked to her last night, and she's having so much fun in Palo Alto, she's thinking about starting a cleaning service there until school starts."

"I'm sorry, David," I said as I rubbed his shoulder.

"That's all right. It was bound to happen sooner or later. She wasn't going to be here that much longer anyway."

"That's the spirit. I've got a feeling there a few girls around town ready to step into Annie's shoes."

"I don't know about that," David said. "Carolyn, could you do me a favor?"

"Anything short of giving you a kidney," I replied.

"It's nothing that dire. I haven't told Mom yet, and I'd appreciate it if you didn't mention it."

"I didn't realize she was that attached to Annie," I said, the understatement of the year.

"It's not that. If she thinks I need a new girlfriend, she'll try to pick one out herself, and I'd kind of like to have a say in it, if you know what I mean."

"I won't say a word," I said. "Are you about ready to take your lunch break?"

"Honestly, I'm not all that hungry. Would you mind going first today?"

"Let me grab my purse and I'm out of here," I said as we both ducked back inside the shop.

"I'm glad I didn't have to twist your arm," David said.

"I try to be flexible when it comes to my employees," I said. "I'll be at Shelly's if anybody needs me. Can I pick up something for you while I'm there?"

"No, Suzy's coming back a little later, and we're going to get a bite. It's not a date or anything," he protested before I could say anything. "It's just lunch."

"Have fun," I said as I left the shop. David appeared to be coming to grips with Annie's early departure quite nicely. Ah, the joys of a young heart that can quickly mend. I wished Rose would bounce back that fast, but I knew that was a false hope. She was mired in a pattern of dating men that weren't right for her, and I wondered if she'd ever be able to break the cycle. I'd known people like her all my life, wasting their lives chasing dreams that would never materialize, many having several choices they were too blind to see themselves. Love could do strange things to people, and for the thousandth time, I was glad I'd found Bill.

I was still wondering about Rose when I heard a gruff voice behind me calling out my name.

It was Rick Cobb, and judging from the

fire in his eyes, I didn't think he was hurry-
ing toward me to offer to take me to lunch.

CHAPTER 10

"Butt out of my life, lady," he said as he neared me. I thought about ducking back into the shop, but what good would that do? I wasn't going to ask David to defend me. I was a grown woman. I could take care of myself.

"I'm sorry. Were you under the impression that I needed your permission to live my life the way I choose to? If I want to dig into other peoples lives, that's my business."

That stopped him for a second. "You're not even going to bother trying to deny it?"

"Why should I? When my husband's under suspicion for murder, your hurt little feelings are not even on my radar screen."

"I don't care who you think you are, Ms. Marbles or somebody like her, but I don't want to hear you've been talking to anybody about me again. Do you understand me?"

I frowned a second, then smiled broadly.

"Okay, now I get it. You lost me for a second there."

"I hope so. I'm not warning you for nothing."

"It's not that," I said. "I was trying to figure out who Ms. Marbles was. You mean Miss Marple of course, don't you, Agatha Christie's delightful character? She's quite a hoot. You should pick up one of her novels sometime."

"I'm not here asking you for a reading list, lady. I'm telling you, stay out of my life." He was doing his best to look ominous, but I refused to give in to his bullying.

"Fine, thanks, I consider myself warned. Now if you'll excuse me, I'm late for lunch."

I looked back at him as I turned the corner, and he was still staring quizzically after me. If that was the best he could do to try to scare me off, he needed lessons in how to pressure people. How could a man who had been so intimidating in his bar be so ineffective out of it? I didn't know if it was the bright sunshine of the day or the familiar confines of the walkway in front of my shop, but his abrupt declarations hadn't ruffled me at all. Something else about the conversation struck me as odd, but I had walked all the way to Shelly's before I figured out what it was. He hadn't men-

210

tioned his brother's death, though I'd brought up the fact that my husband was under suspicion for the man's murder. A glaring omission indeed, as Miss Marple might say. Or Ms. Marbles, for that matter. I didn't like Rick Cobb, but I couldn't let that cloud my judgment. Could he have killed his own brother, his closest living relative? Was there anybody on earth really that heartless? I knew better than to even ask that question. When it came to money and greed, there was no telling about human nature. For some folks, two million dollars wouldn't be enough, not when there was a chance to have four million, no matter what it took to get it.

"You look like you just swallowed a bug," Shelly said as I walked into the diner.

"I didn't swallow one, but I just saw one I would have liked to swat," I said.

"Who was he?" she asked, ignoring the crowd of diners around her. "I'd be glad to pin his arms for you while you smack him." Shelly was a law unto herself when it came to her café, and I pitied the patron who grew impatient with her and demanded immediate attention. I was fairly certain it wouldn't be the kind of notice they'd enjoy.

"Rick Cobb," I said as I took a seat at the counter.

"I could tell you stories about that man that would curl your toes," she said. "In my opinion, he could use a good swatting."

A burly truck driver with a backward baseball cap approached Shelly gingerly. "Sorry to bother you, but I'll leave this here for you."

"Now, Curtis, what did I teach you about interrupting me when I'm talking? You can't be in that big a hurry."

"Shelly, I've got a load of perishables. I did apologize." He looked at her warily as she decided his fate.

"Go on, then, but next time you need to give yourself more of a cushion if you're going to come in here to eat."

"Yes, ma'am, I will. Thanks again. It was delicious, as always."

After he was gone, Shelly said, "Curtis is a good man, but it's taken me a while to train him."

"If you've been so hard on him, what keeps bringing him back?"

Shelly arched one eyebrow. "You mean besides my obvious charms, don't you?"

"That part was so apparent I didn't think I even had to mention it," I said.

She smiled that devilish little smile of hers. "The man is addicted to my pies. He must eat four whole pies a week all by himself.

It's a good thing he's local so he always has access to my offerings, or I'm afraid he'd shrivel up and wither away on the vine."

I'd had a good look at Curtis, and I doubted a seven-year famine would shrivel him up, but I wasn't going to contradict Shelly, especially before I got my food.

She turned her attention back to me. "Did you come here to eat, or are you just admiring the scenery?" she asked me.

"I'm starving," I admitted. "Give me the special. I don't even care what it is."

"I'll have one ready for you in a minute," she said. "In the meantime, here's some tea."

She poured me a glass, then went to wait on the customers who had preceded me. I was wondering if I could stretch my lunch hour to include a little investigative work when someone took the seat beside me. It was Katelynn Gray, a woman I knew well enough to nod to at the grocery store, but not to have over to my house for dinner.

"I heard you talking about a Cobb. Which brother were you discussing?"

"At the moment, I'm interested in both of them," I said.

"Charlie was the nice one, I can tell you that," she said firmly. She seemed to be keeping her voice low, perhaps so word of our talk wouldn't get back to Rick.

"So you've had some experience with the bartender brother," I said. "He's quite a charmer, isn't he?"

Katelynn looked up and down the counter, then said, "I normally don't like to admit it, but I dated him for seven months."

"You must have gotten a medal, lasting that long," I said.

Katelynn bit her lip. "I wanted to leave a lot sooner than that, but I was afraid of him. The only way a woman can get rid of Rick is when he's finished with her."

That sounded serious. "So, you didn't leave him?"

"Like I said, I tried," she said, "but he wouldn't let me."

"I don't suppose you got a restraining order."

She nodded sadly. "He tore it up in my face. I was going to tell the sheriff, but Rick told me he'd see me dead if I did it. Tell your friend Rose she's lucky he got tired of her so quickly."

I studied Katelynn a moment, then said, "I will. I'm just sorry you had to go through it."

"That makes two of us."

She slid off the stool and out the door. A few seconds later, Shelly approached with a plate in her hand. "Here you go: meatloaf, mashed potatoes, and green beans." As she put the plate in front of me, she said softly, "I'm guessing that Katelynn just told you about Rick."

"She did. How on earth did you know that? Were you eavesdropping on my conversations again?"

"Anything said here is fair game as far as I'm concerned, but I didn't need to listen in to know what she was talking about."

It struck me that Shelly had done nothing to mask the subject of our earlier discussion. "You knew all about it, didn't you? That's why you made it a point to talk about Rick so loudly."

"I wanted to give Katelynn the chance to tell you herself. She's had a rough time of it, and I thought talking about it might do her some good."

"And help me, too, in the process. Thanks. Anybody else here I should talk to?"

"Just eat your lunch," she said.

"Yes, ma'am. You don't have to tell me twice."

After I finished my meal and paid for it, I walked back outside and toward Fire at Will. I'd taken just a few steps when I felt someone was behind me. When I twirled around, I was surprised to see Jackson Mallory approaching.

"Hang on a second," he said, nearly out of breath. "Didn't you hear me calling you?"

"No, I was lost in my thoughts," I said. "What do you want, Jackson?"

"Now is that any way to talk to a former suitor?" he asked.

"That was a lifetime ago," I said, "and my lunch hour's almost over. If you've got something to say, spit it out. I'm listening."

"I was hoping we could have a little chat. Since you've already had your lunch, we could make it dinner tonight instead."

"I eat with my husband at night," I said stiffly.

"Fine, I understand. It doesn't hurt to ask."

I looked pointedly at my watch. "As I said, I'm pressed for time right now."

"Then how about if I walk you back to your pottery shop? We can talk as we go."

"I suppose that would be all right," I said. I'd wanted to do a little more digging into Charlie Cobb's murder, but Jackson was still one of my suspects.

"It's a fine day, isn't it?" he said as we started on our way.

I agreed and was tempted to ask him again to get to the point, but I held back. If Jackson had something to tell me, I knew from our history together that he'd have to work up to it himself. When we reached Fire at Will, though, I was still no closer to finding out why the man had asked to talk to me. Trying to hide my impatience, I said, "Jackson, this has been a pleasant walk, but was there something specific you wanted to tell me?"

"Yes, but let's talk about it inside," he said.

Was he serious? "Jackson, I've got work to do."

"You think I can take off whenever I feel like it, Carolyn? This is as important to you as it is to me."

He certainly had my attention. David came outside and said, "Is anything wrong?"

"No, I'm fine."

Before I could ask him to stick around, he said, "I've got to go. I've got a lunch date, remember?"

"I thought it wasn't a date," I said.

"You know what I mean."

Jackson followed me into the shop, and I wondered how I'd managed to get myself in the dubious position of being alone with one of my murder suspects. I grabbed a sharp-pointed tool we used for shaping clay. It didn't look like that formidable a weapon, but I knew I could do some real damage with it if I had to.

217

"Now that we're in here where we won't be disturbed, I can talk to you."

"Customers come in all the time," I said as I grasped the makeshift weapon behind my back. "As a matter of fact, I've got a group that should be here in two minutes."

"I'll make it quick, then."

He reached into his coat pocket, and I tensed, ready to strike. Instead of a gun or a knife, though, Jackson pulled an envelope from his jacket and held it out to me.

"What's that?" I asked suspiciously.

"Open it and see."

I used the tool to cut the envelope open, and I saw ten hundred-dollar bills inside. When I looked up at Jackson, he was smiling.

"I don't get it."

"It's a favor. Now I need one from you."

"I'm not sure what you mean."

He smiled, but I could feel the edge to it. "Think about it. I'm not asking much. Just stick to your pottery and stop digging into Charlie Cobb's unfortunate accident."

"I don't see how you can say that drowning in a bucket of clay slip was an accident." I shoved the money back into his hands.

"Call it what you want, but I didn't have anything to do with it," he said as he refused the money.

"Then why are you trying to buy me off?" I couldn't believe the nerve of the man, attempting to bribe me in my own shop.

"Let's just say I don't want certain things coming to light. Not murder, just a little grease I've used a few times in the past. It's a fair request, and you'll be well compensated for leaving me off your list."

"I don't know why you're even worried about me. It's not like I have any influence with the sheriff, or anyone else in town for that matter."

Jackson picked up a vase in the display and studied it as he said, "Everyone knows Hodges is just putting his time in until he can retire. I figure if anybody's going to find the skeletons in my closet, it's going to be you."

I shoved the money in his hand again, and this time he didn't fight me on it. "Whatever happens, happens."

"Fine," he said, not at all as peeved as I expected him to be after my rejection. The phone rang, and I reached for it as I said, "Now if you'll excuse me, I've got work to do."

"So do I," he said as he walked out of the shop.

It was Butch on the line. "Are you okay?"

"Yes, why do you ask?"

"I just ran into David. He said Jackson Mallory was there when he left. I gave him grief for taking off and leaving you alone like that, so don't worry, it won't happen again."

"I'm a grown woman. I can take care of myself," I said.

"Sure, but even I need help now and then."

"I find that hard to believe." I walked to the window and looked out. For some reason, I had the feeling that Jackson was there, waiting for something. There was no sign of him, but I did find some evidence of his visit in the display window. He'd put the vase back in its rightful place, but underneath it was the envelope he'd tried to force on me. "You know what? Maybe you should come by after all. I could use a hand with something."

"I'll be there in two minutes," he said. I'd get Butch to return the money for me. I knew he could be a lot more persuasive than I was, and I had a feeling Jackson wouldn't be able to say no to him as easily as he had to me.

Butch thumbed through the stack of bills after he got to the shop, but his reaction surprised me. "You can do what you want, but if it were me, I'd keep it."

"You'd take a bribe from that man to look the other way?"

Butch held up his hand. "Now I didn't say that, did I? Just because you take the money doesn't mean you have to do what he wants you to do."

I frowned at him. "That's not honest, is it?"

"And bribing you is? Come on, Carolyn, it's the way he thinks. Every time Jackson runs into a problem, he tries to buy someone off. Consider it a compliment."

"I think it's an insult. I can't believe he thought he could pay me to ignore him."

Butch fanned the money in front of me. "At least he realized you wouldn't come cheap. Tell you what I'd do if I were you. Keep digging, and if it turns out Jackson did it, you can send the money to him in prison. If he didn't kill Charlie Cobb, I'd put it in the Carolyn Emerson Fun Fund. Surely you've got one of those, don't you?"

"Yes, but I don't want to taint it with this money." I took the bills from Butch and threw them on the table. He wasn't taking this seriously enough for my taste.

He thought about it a second, then said, "I've got another idea. Instead of keeping it, why don't you offer some kind of program in the autumn to kids who can't afford to come in here on their own? It could be a kind of scholarship fund."

"I don't know. It's a good idea, but does the end really justify the means?"

Butch shook his head. "I'm not walking into that one. Let the philosophers hash that out. I'm just an ordinary guy."

"I know better than that." I collected the bills, then handed them to him. "Why don't you take this money until I can figure out what I want to do with it?"

He looked startled by the suggestion. "You trust me with this much cash?"

"Why shouldn't I?"

He grinned. "The fact that I used to be a crook comes immediately to mind, doesn't it?"

"The key phrase there is 'used to be.' I know you wouldn't cheat me. We're friends."

"I'm honored by the designation, and the faith you put in me." It was as serious as I'd ever seen him.

"You're most welcome. Since you're here, there is something you can do for me."

"Just name it," Butch said.

"Rick Cobb threatened me on the sidewalk an hour ago."

Butch's fists clenched. "Now that's something in my area of expertise. I'd be happy to straighten him out for you, Carolyn."

I put a hand on his shoulder. "I don't want you to retaliate. I'd love it if you could ask him some questions for me. He doesn't seem all that receptive to me."

"What would you like to know?"

I thought about it a minute, then said, "If he's got an alibi for when his brother was killed, I could strike him off my list. If he doesn't, I'd like to know what he's been up to. As soon as he gets his inheritance, he's leaving town. Can you find out for me?"

"Don't give it another thought," he said. "I'm on it."

I stopped him at the door. "Butch? No rough stuff, okay?"

"I guess that's up to him, isn't it? I'll talk to you later."

After he was gone, I wondered if I'd done the right thing nudging Butch toward Rick Cobb, but it was too late now. Knowing my friend, he'd have something in motion before I'd be able to call it off.

I had no idea how long David would be at lunch with Suzy, but I had enough walk-in customers to keep me busy. Two and a half hours after he'd left, my assistant came rushing back into Fire at Will.

"Carolyn, I'm so sorry I'm late. We lost track of time."

"Then you had a good time?"

David grinned. "Okay, maybe I was wrong. Now that I think about it, that sure felt like a date."

"Have you and Annie discussed your relationship? Does she know it's over?"

He frowned as he tightened the hair in his ponytail. "She's the one who's leaving. It doesn't make sense for us to try to stay together when she'll be all the way across the country."

I touched his arm. "David, I understand what you're saying. But Annie needs to hear these things from you before you start going out with other women, don't you think?"

He frowned. "That's the thing. I never planned on dating anyone so soon, but Suzy is really special."

"I'm happy for you, but you need to deal with Annie first, no matter how painful it might be."

He stared at the floor. "Yeah, I know you're right. I don't want to be one of those guys."

I laughed. "David, my friend, you couldn't be one of those guys if you tried. Now tell me about your lunch."

"We talked for two hours after we ate. It's amazing how much we have in common."

"That sounds nice," I said. "Are you ready to work now?"

"Absolutely." He glanced at the open shelves that surrounded the paint-your-own section. "You've been busy."

"There's been a steady flow. I've got two kilns working now, so we should be in good shape."

The phone rang, and I reached for it. "Fire at Will."

"Carolyn, it's Sandy. I've been doing a little digging, and I found something you should know about."

"What is it?" Sometimes I forgot that while I was going about my pottery business, I had the Firing Squad working on things for me out in the real world.

"Jackson Mallory's had an awful lot of projects pushed through in the last nine months, so I got kind of suspicious. When I started poking around, I found out about the roof collapsing on a project on Green Mountain Lane. Did you hear about it?"

"I remember reading about it in the paper. Someone was hurt, right?"

"A construction worker was killed. He died a day after the accident, and Jackson was the contractor. Take three guesses who the inspector was?"

"The dear, departed Charlie Cobb," I said.

"That's good — you only needed one guess. But do you have any idea who the fatality was?"

"I can't remember the name," I admitted.

"Bob Halloway."

"Should I recognize the name?"

"I didn't, either, until I saw the list of pallbearers at the funeral. He was Nate Walker's wife's third cousin."

"That doesn't sound like all that close a connection," I said.

"I just thought it was interesting," Sandy said. "You never know what something might mean."

"Thanks for the call." I didn't know whether it was significant, but I'd file it away for the next time I talked to Nate. It would be interesting to get his reaction.

To my surprise, my husband, Bill, showed up ten minutes before closing time. "What are you doing here?" I asked him.

"That's a fine way to greet your husband. I hope you do better with your customers, or you'll be out of business in a month."

"I'm just surprised to see you, that's all. I thought you were working."

He shook his head as he frowned. "I can't focus. This afternoon I nearly cut my thumb off on the table saw, so I decided maybe I should be doing something else. Hodges came by to see me this afternoon at my shop."

"What did he want?" My distinct dislike for the sheriff had done nothing but intensify over the past few months. It seemed that every time I turned around, he was accusing me or someone I cared about of murder.

"I think the fool's expecting me to confess to killing Charlie Cobb. Can you believe that?"

"Nothing that man does surprises me."

David walked up front from the back where he'd been working on a new set of vases for our display. "Hey, Bill, I didn't hear you come in."

"Focused on that art, no doubt." Bill was an artisan in his own way, much like David, and the two had formed a bond between wood and clay.

"I try. Carolyn, I need to scoot. I know I owe you some time, but I was hoping I could come in on my day off and make some up."

"That's fine," I said.

David grabbed his jacket, and I said, "David, remember what we talked about."

"I'm going to take care of it the second I get home. Thanks."

"You're welcome," I said.

After he was gone, Bill asked, "What was that about?"

"David's got problems with his love life. I suppose you could call it a problem. Annie's leaving for college, and there's another young lady waiting in the wings to take her place."

Bill grinned. "I remember problems like that."

"So, which was I? Did you have someone stashed away as your backup, or was that my role?"

He took me in his arms and hugged me. "Nobody could take your place, and you know it, so stop fishing around for compliments. Let's grab a few steaks and grill out tonight. What do you say?"

My husband loved to fiddle with his charcoal grill, and I was always delighted when he offered to cook anything that wasn't breakfast themed. "You've got a deal. We can go by the store on the way home. Should we take the truck or my car?"

"It'd be kind of hard to ride home in the truck, since it's back at the house."

I looked at him and asked, "Then how did you get here? Don't tell me the sheriff brought you into town to question you? He's gone too far. We need to find a way to have him removed from office."

Bill chuckled. "Take it easy. Before you plan your coup, you should probably know that I walked here from the house."

"Are you trying to tell me that you exercised? On purpose?"

"I needed some fresh air. It's not that far, and I've done it before. Stop making such a fuss."

"Don't get me wrong, I think it's great." I knew my husband must be troubled if he chose a long walk to clear his head. The sheriff's scrutiny must have been weighing on him more than he was willing to admit. I'd have to crank up the efforts of the Firing Squad and see if we could bring our investigation to a head.

He glanced toward the back. "How are you managing without a bathroom?"

"So far it's just a little inconvenient, but I don't know how long I can wait before I get it back."

Bill nodded. "I was over at the inspector's office, and they treated me like some kind of villain. I'm not sure when we're going to be able to finish it."

"Don't worry. We'll manage. Let's take care of finding the murderer first, and then we'll deal with our plumbing problems."

He nodded, but I knew that it was one more thing troubling my husband. Our lives lately seemed to be a series of loose ends, and it would be nice to tie one or two up before they overwhelmed us.

An hour later, Bill was out back fiddling with the charcoal, and I was inside making a salad and trying not to laugh at his intense focus on getting the perfect pyramid of briquettes, when the telephone rang.

"Hello," I said as I tucked the telephone into the crook of my shoulder so I could still work.

"Carolyn, it's Butch. Do you have a second?"

"Sure. What's up, Butch?"

"I just had a talk with Rick Cobb, and I thought you'd like to know what I found out."

"That was fast."

"What can I say? He was eager to talk to me."

"I can't imagine under what circumstances he'd be willing to share anything with anybody. You didn't have to rough him up, did you?"

"Carolyn, I keep telling you, you've seen too many gangster movies and read too many mystery novels. I didn't lay a finger on him. Well, not a hand. Okay, maybe a hand, but my boots were nowhere near him."

He was making fun of me; it was clear in his voice. Besides, Butch was right. I couldn't very well give him a set of guidelines on his behavior when he was doing something purely as a favor to me. "I get it: don't ask, don't tell. What did he say?"

"Mostly he backed up what you told me. He was dating Rose, but he dumped her the second his brother died. The guy's a real piece of work, isn't he? A lawyer told him he'd get every dime after his brother died, but he swore he didn't know that before Charlie was murdered."

"And you believe him?"

"Let's just say I had no reason not to. By the time we got to that part, he was pretty much willing to tell me whatever I asked him. I think the extra windfall came as a surprise to him. Besides, there was something in his voice when he talked about his brother that made me think Rick actually liked the guy. They were tighter than what folks have been saying. I still have some doubts about him, but what can I say? I don't really have an answer for you."

"Then what's your gut telling you? Is he innocent?" I asked as I finished making the salad.

"I'm nowhere near ready to say that. I just

thought you should know my general impression of the guy."

"Thanks, Butch. I appreciate your help on this."

"Not a problem, Carolyn. You know that. I've got to go. There's something I have to do in Boston that I can't miss."

"It's nothing illicit, is it? Butch, I worry about you."

He chuckled. "You don't have to. My uncle's flying in from Virginia. He's got a layover in Boston, and we're grabbing some dinner and catching up on old times."

"What's he do, or shouldn't I ask?"

"I'm not ashamed of him, even though he is the black sheep of the family."

"Is he a criminal, too?" I asked before the impact of the words hit me. "Wait a second. I didn't mean it like that."

Butch said affably, "You'll need to say something a lot worse than that to get me upset. No, Uncle Pat didn't go into any of the family businesses. He went to law school, if you can believe that."

"And that made him the black sheep in your family?"

"You should see my family." Butch laughed.

After we hung up, Bill walked back inside. "Who was that on the telephone?"

"Butch has been doing some investigating for me," I admitted.

Normally Bill hated it when I poked my nose into police business, but he was remarkably silent at the moment, now that his neck was on the line.

"Is there anything I can do to help you?" he said after a second's hesitation.

"No, there's nothing I can think of. I've got a good team put together, and between us all, we have Maple Ridge pretty much covered."

Bill nodded. "I just feel so helpless about all of this."

I hugged him. "Don't worry. We're going to get through this."

"Yeah, I know you think so. The coals are just about ready." He grabbed the steaks and took them out to the grill while I set the table. I wasn't sure what my next step should be, now that Butch had given a mixed review. That didn't mean the bartender was innocent, but for now I was going to go with Butch's general impression. As for Rose, I believed her when she told me that she hadn't been dating Charlie, and if that was the case, she didn't deserve to be under my scrutiny for murder, unless I was ready to believe she killed the man so her lover would finally have enough money to marry her. Right now, that idea was too far out there to consider.

That left Jackson and Nate on my suspect list, and with Nate's secondary connection to the dead building inspector, it was time I spoke with the coffee shop owner again. It would wait until morning, though. For now, I was going to enjoy a quiet dinner at home with my husband.

At least I hoped it would be quiet.

CHAPTER 11

"Carolyn, if you keep coming in this early, I'm going to have to put you on the payroll." Nate Walker was in a chipper mood, in direct opposition to my own. I wasn't getting enough sleep, and the night before, Bill had gotten me sucked into a movie that I had to see the ending of. Hannah was leaving for Italy later today, so yet again, I'd given myself plenty of time to talk to Nate. Maybe too much.

"I'm not here just for the coffee, even though I love it," I said. "Nate, we need to talk again. I'm not happy with the way we left things yesterday."

"Now why do you have to go and ruin a perfectly good morning like that?"

There were a few other early birds in the coffee shop but not enough to require any attention from the owner.

"The sooner you ease the suspicions around you, the faster I get off your back and move on to somebody else," I said, probably a little more honestly than I should have.

"I guess that's worth a few minutes of my time. Carolyn, for somebody without any official police standing, you surely do manage to make a lot of waves in this little town."

"What can I say? It's a gift. Would you like to join me at a table, or should we go outside again?"

"Let's go over here," he said, pointing to a table that was out of the way. "But keep your voice down, okay? I don't want the world knowing my business."

"That's fine with me," I said. Hopefully we'd be able to get through this without too many fireworks.

"So, what do you want to know. I've thought a lot about it, and I'm willing to talk to you now."

"Let's start with Bob Halloway."

He looked truly surprised by the reference. "Winnie's cousin? What about him?"

At least Nate hadn't tried to deny knowing him. "How well did you know him? I understand you were a pallbearer at his funeral."

Nate nodded. "They had trouble getting enough guys, so I stepped in at the last second. It was no big deal. We weren't all that close, but it was kind of a family duty I was willing to perform."

"And you don't hold any resentment about the way he died?"

Perplexed, Nate replied "Carolyn, what does that have to do with anything?" Before I could say anything, he said suddenly, "Wait a second. You don't think Bob's death had anything to do with Charlie's murder, do you? I told you, I hardly knew the guy, and what I did know, I didn't care that much about. He was loud, and he had a habit of telling the most inappropriate jokes in all of the wrong places. We'd lost touch after Winnie died. To answer your question, no, I didn't kill Charlie Cobb to avenge my dead wife's cousin. Was that it?"

He started to get up, and I put a hand on his arm. "No, there's something else. I understand the sheriff spent some time investigating you just after your wife's death."

Nate's face went rigid as I said it, and I knew I'd pushed him a little too far yet again.

"What do you want to know?" His words were icy.

"What really happened the night Winnie died?"

Nate just shook his head. "You know what? I just changed my mind. I won't talk about that ever again, not with you and not with anybody else."

When he stood this time, I made no move to stop him. What if the guy was innocent in all of this? How would I feel if I were in his shoes? I had to be careful. Nate deserved that much at least.

He walked around the counter, and I left the coffee shop. That was the last questioning session I was ever going to have with Nate if I could help it. If he was hiding something, he was too good at it for me. And if he wasn't, I didn't want to push the man into the past any more than I already had. His memories of his wife were all he had left of her, and I wasn't about to diminish them in his eyes.

"There you are," Hannah said when she walked into Fire at Will an hour later. There were two coffee cups in her hands. "You stood me up again."

In my haste to get away, I'd completely forgotten about her. "I'm so sorry."

Hannah handed me a cup. "I understand you and Nate had a little chat this morning."

"He told you that?" I asked, then took a

sip of coffee.

"No, but one of his employees did. It appears the man has departed the premises yet again. You seem to have that effect on him lately, according to the cashier."

"What can I say? It's a talent I rarely use, repelling men."

"What did you two talk about this time? Wait, I don't want to know. The last thing I need in my life is to get dragged into your little hit squad."

"It's called the Firing Squad, and you know it."

"Fine, call it what you will, but you and your little group leave quite a wake around town. You seem to leave bruised feelings wherever you go."

I frowned. "Do I sense a hint of criticism in your voice?"

"Me? Never. It must just be your imagination."

"Hannah, when Bill's freedom and his reputation are at stake, I'll ruffle as many feathers as I have to so I can clear his name," I said, despite my reservations about pushing Nate again. Hannah didn't have to know about that.

She nodded. "I know how you are, Carolyn. I'd expect nothing less from you." Hannah looked around the shop. "Where's my son this morning?"

I glanced at the clock and realized that he should have been in ten minutes earlier. "He must be on the late shift today."

"And that's something you don't know about? What's he been up to lately?"

No way on earth I was going there with her. The best way to answer her inquiry was to meet her with another question, as many times as I could get away with it. "Why do you ask?"

She frowned. "I don't know. He seemed particularly happy after work yesterday."

"That's a good thing, right?"

"I suppose so. I just wish I knew why." She was troubled, that much was clear.

I knew the reason for David's new and brighter mood, but it wasn't my place to divulge it. "Why don't you ask him yourself?"

"Probably because I'm afraid of the answer I'll get." She moved to the door, then said, "Next time you stand me up, I'm charging the coffee to you."

"That's fair," I said with a grin. "Thanks, Hannah. I'm sorry I missed our usual get-together."

"Please, I'm only teasing. I'll see you when I get back."

"Have a safe trip, but be sure to have fun, too."

"I will," she said.

"Bye."

Two minutes after she was gone, David walked in. "Is the coast clear?"

I tapped my foot on the floor. "David Atkins, are you actually ducking your own mother?"

"Let's just say I need a little more space than she's willing to give me right now," he admitted. "Her time in Italy is something we both need right now."

"Did you talk to Annie?"

He nodded glumly. "That's why I'm late. We were talking until midnight and I didn't get much sleep."

"I take it things didn't go well."

He rubbed his eyes. "You should get a crystal ball. Let's just say I don't have to worry about her looking me up the next time she comes back to town."

I suddenly felt sorry for Annie. "She's hurt, but she'll get over it. You did the right thing."

"I know, but it didn't make breaking it off with her any easier."

I patted his shoulder. "It's tough being a grownup, isn't it?"

"Does it ever get any easier?"

I smiled at him. "Not yet, but I'll be sure to let you know if it ever does."

Jenna came in around lunchtime, but I was with a group of customers and couldn't talk to her right away. I nodded toward her, then held up five fingers to indicate I had five more minutes before I'd be finished. I was helping a group of seven — three adults and four children — paint their own plates. If the application process was any indication of how the finished products would look, I wasn't sure they'd take their pieces of art after they were fired, even though they'd already paid for them. That was why I always insisted on cash up front. A lot of customers never bothered to come back to pick up their wares, or refused to take them once they saw the results. It wasn't that hard to do, decorating a plate, a mug, or a saucer, but some folks seemed to have the knack of ruining them without trying. I didn't have very high hopes for the group at hand.

"Give me a few days," I told them as I held the front door open for the last stragglers, "then you can pick up your pieces."

After they were gone, Jenna said, "That looked like fun."

"Well, appearances can be deceiving," I said as I cleaned the tables and tried to put the paints back in some kind of order. "I'm not sure what they're going to say once they see the finished products, but at least they had a good time doing them. What brings you by?"

"Can't I just come to work on a project of my own?"

"Of course you can," I said as I washed my hands. I had to scrub all the way to my elbows, though truthfully, that wasn't an unusual occurrence at my shop. "What would you like to do?"

"Take you out to lunch," she said.

"What about making something here first?"

"I was teasing, Carolyn. Can you get away for a bit? I was thinking about going to the Waterfront."

The Waterfront was a restaurant that was out of my price range on a good day, and there was no way I could pay for my meal without forgoing some other luxury, like water or electricity. "Thanks, but I'm not sure I have that much time."

"Did I mention that it was my treat?" she asked with a smile.

"No, you failed to give me that piece of pertinent information. Why the largesse?"

She came close to me and said softly, "I just inherited some money, and I wanted to share the celebration with a friend. Trust me, today I can afford it."

"I'm not exactly dressed for it," I said, staring down at my blue top and khakis.

"You look fine. The lunch crowd there is always dressed casually."

If she didn't mind how I looked, then I wouldn't, either. "If you're sure," I said.

"You're the first person I thought of."

"I find that hard to believe. Don't worry, I don't mind if Butch was busy." I grinned at her, waiting for her to deny it. The sparks had been flying between the two of them for some time, and I kept wondering when they'd act on them.

She didn't answer me directly, which was a sure giveaway, in my book. Instead, she smiled lightly, then said, "Perhaps you were the second, but at least you made the list."

"So what happened with Butch?"

Jenna shrugged. "He couldn't make it. No matter how much he protested that he'd love to accompany me, I had the distinct feeling the Waterfront was not his idea of an enjoyable place to dine."

"He's got a few rough edges, but give him time. He's getting better by the day."

"So you say," Jenna said. "Would you like to come, or must I go to the third name on my list?"

"I'd be delighted to join you," I said, matching the formality of her invitation. I didn't even want to know who that third person was. "David, could you come here a second?"

He joined us from the back. "What's up, boss? Hi, Jenna."

"Hello, David."

"I'm taking a long lunch," I told him. "I trust you're fine with that."

"After I didn't show up on time this morning? You can take the rest of the day off as far as I'm concerned."

The idea hadn't crossed my mind, but suddenly, that was exactly what I wanted. "You've got a deal. You know how to close up. I'll see you tomorrow."

He looked surprised, since I was almost always there at closing time. "Are you serious?"

"Do I look like I'm joking? I trust you, David. You should know that by now."

"Of course I do," he said. "Have a good time."

I hesitated at the door. "David, I didn't even think to ask you if were feeling up to it. Will you be all right?"

"Absolutely. Now go, and don't give the shop a second thought."

"We won't," Jenna said as she put her arm

through mine and we left Fire at Will.

The restaurant could have been used in a photo shoot for New England elegance. Bone china adorned each table setting, and vases of freshly cut flowers graced the room like individual gardens. The white linen tablecloths gleamed in the sunlight coming in through the plate glass windows overlooking the river, and I tried to capture the images in my mind to savor later.

After we were seated, I studied the menu and had to catch my breath when I saw the prices.

Whispering so no one around us could hear, I asked, "Are you sure about this?"

Jenna smiled. "Please, you are my guest. Choose whatever you'd like."

"If you don't mind me asking, who exactly did you get this inheritance from?"

"I don't mind telling you at all," Jenna said. "My aunt Rita passed away, and since no one on the planet could stand being around her, she left her money to me, some sort of consolation prize for putting up with her over the years, I suppose."

I hadn't been expecting that as an explanation. "Was she really that bad?"

"Carolyn, you have no idea. She was not just stingy with her money. She was stingy with her love. I don't know what made her such a bitter old woman, but from what I've heard, she was born with a clod of dirt in her mouth. The woman acted as though she'd be charged a hundred dollars every time she smiled. When the funeral director showed me her final repose, complete with a slight smile, I made them do it over until she wore the scowl I'd seen my entire life."

"She sounds like she was miserable."

Jenna nodded. "I believe Abraham Lincoln said that people were just about as happy as they made up their minds to be, and I couldn't agree with him more."

"So why are we here celebrating, then?"

Jenna smiled slightly. "Because Aunt Rita wouldn't have approved of me squandering part of my inheritance on a nice meal out."

"Should we be doing it, then?"

"Are you kidding? If she's watching us — looking up, not down, let me assure you — she's fussing and fuming, which always made her happy when she was alive. So eat up, enjoy yourself, and we'll toast the sour old bird with every drink." Jenna studied the menu. "I'm having the duck. How about you?"

"I'll have the salmon, if you're sure."

"You can do better than that, can't you? Come on, live a little, Carolyn."

"Maybe I'll have dessert, too," I said reluctantly.

"That's the spirit." Jenna waved to the waitress standing discreetly by. "We're ready now."

After we placed our orders and were served glasses of champagne, Jenna held hers up to me. "To enjoying life, and to Rita."

"To Rita," I echoed, then we tapped our flutes and drank.

The food was even better than its reputation. I planned to start saving for a return visit as soon as I got back to the shop. Maybe if I scrimped and saved for eight or nine years, I'd be able to come back. If Bill wanted to join me, we'd probably have to wait even longer.

Dessert was out of this world — a chocolate mousse and cake concoction that made my teeth hurt to look at. I knew exactly where every calorie I swallowed would end up, but I didn't care. It was nothing short of extraordinary, and all of it was pure indulgence.

We were having coffee after our meal, and Jenna was waiting on her change from the check, though I doubted there'd be anything left of the two crisp, new hundred-dollar bills she'd handed over.

"How lovely," I said, content beyond all belief. "Thanks so much for including me."

"You were the perfect guest," she said.

We were ready to go, so we walked out to Jenna's car. She'd been gracious enough to drive us to the restaurant, and now I was glad I'd taken her up on her offer. I was so stuffed I wasn't sure I'd be able to fit behind my own steering wheel.

I was buckling my seat belt when Jenna said suddenly, "Duck down."

"Why?" I asked.

"Just do it."

I released the belt, then slouched down in my seat. "Why exactly are we doing this?" I asked.

"Look over there."

I peeked up over the dashboard and looked in the direction she'd pointed.

Jackson Mallory was getting out of his car, but that wasn't the surprising part of the view.

He was escorting Rose Nygren to lunch, and the two of them looked like they'd been close forever. There was something comfortable about the way he put his arm around her waist to steady her, and the way Rose leaned into him as she spoke.

Once they were inside the restaurant, I sat back up in my seat and asked Jenna, "What on earth was that about?"

"They looked like they were up to something, didn't they? I thought Rose was still pretty upset over Charlie Cobb's death. Didn't she just break up with his brother, Rick? That's a pretty quick rebound."

"She didn't act the part of a jilted lover just now, did she?" I asked.

"That's not what I was seeing, either," Jenna said. "Do you suppose there's a chance the two of them just got together?"

"I doubt it. They looked entirely too chummy to me. But what does it mean?"

"I don't have a clue, unless Rose is leading some kind of secret life nobody knows about."

I thought about that for a few seconds, then said, "I'd sure like to know more than I do. I'm going to have to keep a closer eye on Rose."

Jenna started the car. "She's not going to like the idea of you spying on her."

"She's just going to have to deal with it," I said. "I can't really afford to worry about what people think of me at the moment."

Jenna nodded. "I'm sorry she spoiled our outing."

"It's fine. I won't let it bother me. Honestly, I had a lovely time."

"I just can't help feeling that Aunt Rita

had something to do with them showing up like that, haunting me from beyond the grave. It's something she would do, if she has any power in the afterlife. That woman never could leave well enough alone."

After Jenna dropped me off at my car in the parking lot above the River Walk, I wasn't sure what to do. I wanted to talk to Rose about her lunch with Jackson, but they might not be back for hours. So what was I going to do in the meantime? I could go back to Fire at Will, but I'd been given a pass to play hooky for the rest of the day, and while I loved my shop, sometimes it was good to just get away. If I stayed anywhere near the River Walk, I knew I'd run into too many people I knew. Though it was still early afternoon, I decided to go home. Bill wasn't working, at least he hadn't been the last time I'd talked to him. Maybe we could catch a movie, or do something to get away from the cloud hanging over his head.

His truck was in the driveway, but he wasn't in the house. I walked out to his shop and glanced in the window. He was happily working on something, joining two pieces of dark wood in some sort of complicated clamping system. It appeared that Bill had managed to put his troubles aside and lose himself in his work again.

I walked back to the house and turned on a movie. I lost interest quickly, though, and shut it off.

There were so many things troubling me about Charlie Cobb's murder, I couldn't sort them out. After grabbing a legal pad and a pencil, I curled up on the couch and started writing down what I knew. My list of suspects didn't include my husband, though I knew he topped the sheriff's roster of likely candidates. I did list Rick Cobb, despite Butch's gut reaction to the man; Jackson Mallory; and as much as I hated to, Rose Nygren and Nate Walker. Charlie Cobb might have been killed by somebody else, but if he was, they didn't make my list. And if that were the case, it would be up to Sheriff Hodges to figure it out, and that would probably mean that a killer would go free.

I'd read enough mysteries to know that three things were needed to establish a killer: motive, means, and opportunity. Drowning Charlie in a bucket of clay slip hadn't taken as much strength as one might have expected, because whoever had done it had hit him in the head first, from behind. So the real question was how had they lured Charlie into the alley behind my shop in

the first place? I couldn't imagine him going there with a stranger, and that meant he
had known his killer. The blow had come
from behind, so Charlie had been comfortable enough with his murderer to turn his
back on him — or her — a fatal mistake. I
would have loved to ask the coroner for
details of that blow. Had it come from a
downward or an upward swing? Hodges
would know, but I doubted the sheriff
would share that, or any other piece of
information with me. I stood and pretended
to deliver a series of fatal blows to an
imaginary victim in all sorts of positions,
and finally concluded that the angle of
impact probably didn't indicate much about
the murderer. The direction of the blow
would have depended on where Charlie was
when he was struck, and nobody but the
killer had any idea. For instance, if Charlie
had been bent over, say to pick something
up, the blow would have come from above,
though the killer might have been a great
deal shorter than Charlie.

I was still swiping the air with an imaginary brick when I heard a cough behind
me. "Do I even want to know what you're
doing?"

I looked at my husband and said, "I'm
trying to get you off of a murder charge. I

thought you were working in your shop."

"I ran out of clamps, so I have to wait until the joints I glued up are dry before I can go on to the next step. Why aren't you at Fire at Will?"

"I had something more important to do. Come here a second."

He stepped forward. "What is it?"

I threw my pad on the floor in front of me. "Pick that up, would you?"

He looked at me as if I'd just lost my mind. "Why? You dropped it. Pick it up yourself."

"Bill, could you, for once in your life, co-operate and do what I ask?"

He didn't like it, but my husband leaned forward and reached for the pad. As he did so, I swatted him lightly in the head with my open hand. That theory was proven, at any rate.

"Hey, there's no reason to hit me. I was picking it up, just like you asked me to."

"I'm testing an idea," I said. "Now, turn around for a second."

He rubbed his scalp. "Not if you're going to hit me again."

"Stop being such a baby. This is important."

He turned, and I swooped down on him from different angles until I was satisfied that I'd exhausted the possibilities.

When I stopped, Bill said, "That's it. You've finally gone over the edge."

"Anybody could have done it," I said as I shook my head. "This didn't prove anything. How hard do you have to hit somebody with a brick to knock them out?"

He took a step away from me. "I don't know, and I don't intend to find out. You just lost your test dummy."

"I wasn't going to try that on you," I said.

"Well, don't get mad at me for thinking you might."

I sighed. "I was just hoping to eliminate somebody from my list of suspects, but all this proves is that anybody could have killed Charlie Cobb."

Bill sat down heavily in the chair. "I don't know if I'd say that. How mad would you have to be at somebody to hold their face down in a bucket of that mud until they drowned? I for one know that I couldn't do it."

"Neither could I," I replied, then added, "Then again, maybe I could."

He looked shocked. "I hope you're going to explain that to me."

"If somebody did something to you or one of the boys, I might be able to bring myself to murder. I'm not saying I would, but I can't rule it out, either, not if I'm being honest about it."

He nodded. "You've got a point." Bill leaned over and grabbed my pad again. "Let's see what you've got here." As he read the list, I saw him smile.

"What's so funny?"

"I didn't make the roster," he said.

"That's because I couldn't think of a motive for you," I said, adding a slight grin.

"I hope you had more reasons than that to leave me off. So, what motives do the others have?"

I took the pad from him and studied the list. "Rick Cobb's motive could be greed or jealousy."

Bill frowned. "I understand the greed part after what you told me about the will, but jealousy? I thought Rose was dating him, not his brother."

"Both brothers could have been after her; sibling rivalry gone bad. Could she have thought Rick would have enough money to marry her if he inherited his brother's estate?"

Bill looked skeptical. "I don't see Rose Nygren as being capable of that kind of murder."

"I don't, either, but I can't rule her out."

"So we leave her on the list," Bill said. "I

suppose we don't have to look far for a motive for Jackson, do we?"

I hadn't said a word to Bill about the bribe Jackson had given me, and I knew Butch wouldn't have, either. "Why do you say that?"

"Come on. He's the biggest contractor in our part of Vermont, and Charlie Cobb was a building inspector. You have to wonder if a little money passed between them under the table to get Charlie to look the other way. Maybe he started asking Jackson for more, or he could have threatened to shut down Jackson's projects for violations. There's plenty of motive for murder there." He glanced over at my list again. "You've got Nate Walker on your list? Why?"

"Sandy was digging on the Internet and found something that might be a factor. It appears that Charlie Cobb was arrested for DUI around the time Nate's wife was killed by a hit-and-run driver. They never found the guy, but what if Nate learned that Charlie had been the one who killed his wife? That's motive enough."

I saw a shiver go through Bill, and it had nothing to do with the temperature in the house. "I'd hate to see a list of motives like that for people with bad feelings toward me."

"Me, too. That would mean somebody killed you."

"That would be bad, too, but that's not what I meant." He tapped the pad. "It's amazing how many people might have wanted to kill this guy. How can the sheriff focus just on me?"

"He sees only the obvious, and who knows, most of the time, he's probably right. You were the one that half the town saw fighting with Charlie the day he died. Let's face it, that argument wasn't exactly low profile."

"I know I've got a temper. So did Charlie."

I patted my husband's knee. "That's why we're trying to find out who might have done it besides you."

"You know, something just occurred to me. The killer might not even be on that list of yours."

I frowned. "I've considered the possibility, but if it was somebody else, there's nothing either one of us can do about it." I looked down again, then added, "We've covered means and motive, but opportunity is a little tricky. I've tried to ask everybody about their alibis, but nobody's been all that forthcoming with their answers. The problem is that the sheriff has a right to ask them these questions. All I can do is hope one of them tells me something, and then I can try to prove if they're lying to me. It's not easy."

Bill stood and took my hand, pulling me up. "Don't stop trying, okay? I'm counting on you."

It was a tender moment for him, and a rare one at that. As he hugged me, I realized yet again how much this gruff man meant to me. We'd spent nearly thirty years together, and I couldn't imagine my life without him. I was about to tell him just that when he pulled away and said, "I'm starving. What's for dinner?"

"Well, I'm not particularly hungry," I replied. I told him about my lunch with Jenna at the Waterfront, then added, "But I'll be happy to make you something. What would you like?"

"Pot roast would be great, but I don't guess there's time to make one, is there?"

I glanced at the clock. "Not unless you want to eat after midnight."

"Forget that," he said. "Do you have any other ideas?"

I thought about what I had on hand. "I can make meatloaf and mashed potatoes."

"Sold," he said. "Do you want any help?"

That was certainly out of character. I was as likely to help my husband in his workshop as he was to help me in the kitchen. "No, I think I can handle it."

"Good. Those joints should be dry by now, so I want to get started on the next set. Call me when it's time to eat."

I nearly threw the legal pad at him as he left.

Glancing at my list one last time, I imagined each one of my suspects killing Charlie Cobb. I knew in my heart that one of them had, but the worst thing about it was that I could visualize his last minutes of life four different ways, with a different set of hands holding him down each time.

CHAPTER 12

I was just finishing up the dishes after dinner and Bill had already retreated to the workshop again, when the telephone rang. "Carolyn, I'm sorry to bother you at home, but this couldn't wait."

"That's fine, Butch."

"I'm not interrupting your dinner, am I?"

"No, we're done."

"Good. Listen, maybe you should forget what I said about Rick Cobb. I'm not sure I gave you such good advice."

"What changed your mind?" I finished rinsing the meatloaf pan and put it in the rack to dry as I talked.

"I had another chat with him a few minutes ago, and he actually had the nerve to blow me off, if you can believe that."

I couldn't imagine anyone dismissing Butch out of hand. "What did he say?"

"He told me to stay out of his business, or he was going to sic his friends on me."

"Butch, I hope I didn't put you in a dangerous position. Could he know people who might hurt you?"

He laughed so loudly I had to pull the telephone away from my ear. After it subsided, I asked, "What's so funny?"

"The names he mentioned were all friends of mine. It still got my blood boiling that he'd try to threaten me. There was something in his eyes right before I started laughing that I didn't like. I've seen it enough in the past. The guy wanted to kill me, and all I was doing was asking some pretty innocent questions about his brother, and saying how nice it was for him to get the entire inheritance without having to split it with anyone else."

"You don't think that might have antagonized him a little?"

"Carolyn, that's what questioning is all about. I push somebody until they start to push back, or fold on me. Either way, I find out more than I would have before."

"You've got a point," I said as I drained the water in the sink. "But I don't think it's my style."

There was a long pause, then he said, "Tell you what. You leave the intimidation to me, okay?"

"That's a deal. Thanks for calling, Butch."

"You're welcome. I just thought you should know about my change of heart before you wrote Rick Cobb off altogether."

After I hung up the phone, I stared out the window a few seconds, wondering if I should call the rest of the Firing Squad and see if they could do anything else. What could I ask, though? *I* needed to talk to Rose, not delegate it to someone else. As for Rick Cobb, he'd been pushed enough already. That left Jackson Mallory and Nate Walker, but did I really want Jenna or Sandy or Martha talking to them? I counted on my gang of investigators for background work, but I needed to see how the people on my list reacted to my questions in order to guage the truthfulness of their answers.

I had a busy day ahead of me tomorrow, and I thought about tackling one of the three left on my list before bedtime, but I was tired, and I'd had more than my fill of murder for the moment.

Hannah had left for her trip to Italy, so I didn't have to worry about forgetting our morning meeting at the coffee shop the next day. I decided it would be a perfect time to delay my daily visit to In the Grounds. After all, Nate had probably seen more of me than he ever cared to. As I arrived at the shop owned by the first person on my list, I glanced in and saw Rose sitting in a rocking chair, crying again. Her crocodile tears weren't going to work on me this time.

I tapped on the glass, but it took her a few seconds to realize someone was there. She looked up at me, startled, and dabbed furiously at her cheeks before she waved to me.

"Let me in," I said as I motioned to the front door.

It was pretty obvious she was reluctant to do it, but when she saw I wasn't going to just go away, she got up and unlocked the front door. I didn't step inside, and she didn't invite me in, either.

"Rose, what are you crying about this time?"

I could tell that the harshness of my tone surprised her. "Nothing," she said, sniffling into a handkerchief.

"Unless you've got a cold or allergies, that's not true, is it?"

"Oh, Carolyn, I don't know what to do. Nothing's working out like I'd planned." The sobbing started again, but this time I wasn't going to make the mistake of trying to comfort her. I could only take so much drama.

"Rose, pull yourself together." My words snapped out at her like a slap in the face.

She looked shocked. "Carolyn, what's gotten into you?"

"You're a grown woman. If you persist in putting yourself in these situations with inappropriate men, what do you expect the outcome to be? For once in your life, use your head instead of your heart." I hadn't meant my words to be so harsh, but she needed to hear them, and I was in the perfect mood to be the bad messenger.

"It's not as easy as you think," she said, adding a little backbone to her words. Good. Maybe I'd gotten through to her.

"I never said it would be easy. Growing up never is."

"I'm an adult, and I have been for many years."

I shook my head. "I don't care what your driver's license says, I'm talking about your maturity. Honestly, what were you thinking, sneaking around town with Jackson Mallory?"

Every drop of blood must have drained out of her face. "What are you talking about?"

"Maple Ridge isn't all that big a place." I decided not to tell her how inadvertently I'd acquired my knowledge.

"We're just friends. We have been for years. When I needed some comfort, he's always there for me."

I shrugged but didn't say a word. After a few seconds, Rose added, "Yesterday I needed a shoulder to cry on. It was nothing more than that."

"I doubt that. Not after the way I saw the two of you acting." I was pushing it, trying to take Butch's advice on interrogation.

Rose bit her lip. "I admit that I drank a little something before we had lunch. I'm not much of a drinker, so it went to my head I guess. You won't tell anyone, will you?"

"They won't hear it from me," I said. Then it hit me. "Rose, what plan were you talking about a second ago?" I realized that I might have misinterpreted her words. Could the plan have been to kill Charlie so Rick would inherit enough money to marry her? Or was it something more benign, like finding a husband?

"I don't know. I was babbling."

"I'm not so sure of that," I said. "Rick inherited quite a bit from his brother, didn't he?"

Rose's gaze narrowed. "So?"

"I'm just wondering if someone else was counting on that."

For a split second, I saw her pupils dilate. Her tone was stiff as she said, "You shouldn't speculate. Somebody could get hurt."

"Or end up in jail," I said. The old Rose I knew wouldn't have killed someone for love, but I wasn't so sure about the woman standing in front of me. Suddenly, I wasn't all that comfortable standing talking to her without someone backing me up. I glanced at my watch and pretended I was in a hurry. "I've got to go."

As I started to leave, Rose called out, "Where are you going?"

"I'll talk to you later. Good-bye, Rose."

I walked into In the Grounds a few moments later, and the proprietor himself was behind the counter. Nate greeted me, then asked, "Are you waiting for Hannah, or can I get you something?"

"She's not coming," I said. "How about my usual?"

"Coming right up." As he got my coffee, I became painfully aware that we were alone in his shop. "Where is everyone?" I asked.

Nate shrugged. "Some mornings are like this."

What should I do, I asked myself: take advantage of the situation and start questioning him, or take the safe, cowardly way out and get my coffee to go?

"I understand the sheriff thought you

might have run Winnie down yourself," I found myself blurting out. I wasn't sure what had happened to my earlier decision to stop pressuring Nate about what had happened to his wife, but evidently another part of my brain had vetoed it.

He dropped my coffee, and it spilled all over the floor. "Why would you say something like that?" Nate asked, ignoring the puddle of liquid.

"It's the truth, isn't it?"

Nate scowled at me. "He interviewed me and even checked the front fender of my car. There was no damage to it, Carolyn." Nate took a deep breath, then said, "Maybe you should get your morning coffee somewhere else from now on."

"Are you actually banishing me from your shop?" I asked.

"I'm asking you nicely, but if you force the issue, then I guess you could say I am. You're more trouble than you're worth."

He grabbed a mop and ignored me. I stood there for a minute like a prize idiot, then left, without my morning jolt of caffeine. Instant would have to do. At least I had some back at Fire at Will. To my surprise, Jackson was waiting for me by my door.

Without a greeting of any kind, he

snapped, "What did you say to Rose?"

"What business is it of yours?" I asked.

"I told you to stay out of this Charlie Cobb business. I even paid for the privilege, if you recall."

"Come by later and I'll give you a refund," I said. "I don't have time for you right now."

"Make the time," he snapped at me again.

"You're not threatening me, too, are you?" I suddenly felt very vulnerable being outside. It was too early to have many shoppers. In fact, I couldn't see anyone else along the entire River Walk. Even Kendra would be a welcome vision at this point.

"I don't threaten, Carolyn. I deliver. I'm telling you to leave Rose alone."

"Jackson, I thought you two were friends." Rose had been pretty emphatic about it, but that wasn't the signal I was getting from my former boyfriend.

"That's exactly right, not that it's any of your business. Drop this, and I mean now."

He turned and walked off, but my heart didn't ease its pounding until I was on the other side of a locked door. I'd allotted too much time for interviews, so I was in the shop an hour before I was set to open. I thought about unlocking the door early, but the thought of Jackson Mallory out there somewhere lying in wait for me was enough to make me keep it bolted.

I was missing something. I just knew it. Someone had given me something to go on, but I was too distracted by all the possibilities to narrow my choices. I suddenly realized I'd be the world's worst juror, believing whoever spoke from the witness stand. I'd advised Rose to go with her head and not her heart; I decided to take my own advice.

I wrote a note for David to open the shop without me, and walked toward Rose's place.

I never made it, though. Kendra was in front of her shop, and the second she saw me, she started scowling. "If you're looking for Rose, she's not there," Kendra said.

"How do you know?"

"I saw her leave. From the sound of it, you were pretty nasty to her this morning, Carolyn."

I wasn't about to stand there and let Kendra Williams lecture me on manners. "She needed to hear what I had to say. I'm not finished with her, either."

"I think you are. Go look at the note on her door."

I walked over to Rose Colored Glasses and saw a hand-printed sign on the front door. "Closed until further notice," it said, in Rose's spidery hand.

Kendra shouted, "You ran her off, maybe for good." I didn't know how to respond to that. Kendra added, "You should at least have the decency to go tell her you're sorry before she leaves."

"Do you really think she wants to talk to me right now?" Given our earlier conversation, I doubted she'd welcome me if I popped up on her doorstep as she was packing her bags.

"You're probably the only one she'll listen to."

Blast it all, I didn't need this complication, but I didn't want Kendra slamming me all around Maple Ridge, either. Then it hit me. What if I'd come too close to the truth, and Rose was using my warning as an excuse to take off before the sheriff came to the same conclusion and started asking her some hard questions about her involvement with the murder? Had I actually pushed her hard enough to make her escape?

Kendra's voice brought me back to reality. "Are you going over there, or are you just going to stand here all day?"

"I'm going," I said.

"It's about time," she said.

I headed for the Intrigue, and as I walked

along the River Walk, I thought about getting one of my friends from the Firing Squad to back me up, but there wasn't time. If I waited for someone else to show up, Rose might already be gone.

Her car was still in front of her place when I got there. I was having major second and third thoughts about confronting her alone. I sat out in the Intrigue and called Bill, but he must have been in the workshop, because he didn't pick up. I tried Butch next, but he wasn't answering, either. I nearly hung up when his voice mail kicked in, but instead I said, "Butch, it's Carolyn. I'm at Rose Nygren's, and I think there's a chance that she might have killed Charlie Cobb. If you get this, I might need you."

I was ready to call Jenna when Rose came outside, carrying a suitcase in one hand and a garment bag in the other. She threw her clothes in the back of her car, then walked over to me.

I got out, wishing I'd grabbed some kind of weapon to defend myself along the way. Then I realized I had my car keys in my hand. Grasping them in my fist, I let each jagged edge slip out between my clinched fingers. I might not be able to do much damage to her with my makeshift claw, but at least I'd go down swinging.

"What are you doing here?" she asked. "Haven't you done enough damage?"

"We need to talk," I said as calmly as I could manage, hiding my hands behind my back.

"I'm through talking with you. In fact, I think I'm through with this inbred little hamlet that doesn't even deserve a name. I'm leaving."

"You bought your building. How can you just leave?"

"I'll sell it, with everything in it. I have to get away, can't you see that? I need a fresh start somewhere else."

"Are you really that upset, or are you just using this little tantrum as an excuse to get away from Sheriff Hodges?"

No matter how many times I told myself never to poke a bear, I still managed to do it with alarming regularity. Today was clearly no exception. Rose took a step toward me, and I got ready to defend myself. Instead of attacking me, though, I could see the tears welling up in her eyes. "I can't stand it anymore, Carolyn. How does Bill do it? Half the town thinks he's a killer."

"The difference is, most of us know he's not."

"I'm not, either," she shouted. I looked around us, but her street was deserted. Just great. There's never an audience when you need one.

"Take it easy," I said. "Nobody's accusing you of anything."

"No, but you're one breath away. I can hear it in your voice. You should be more like Nate Walker. He's offered me sympathy through this entire mess, not a handful of accusations and innuendoes."

"Nate knew about you and Rick?" I asked. "I thought you were keeping your relationship secret."

Rose said, "We were trying to, but Nate found out. At least he thought he did." Rose frowned, then added, "Funny thing was, he spotted Charlie and me together, and Nate immediately jumped to the wrong conclusion. We were talking about Rick, and Nate thought we were dating instead. It took forever to set him straight, but once I did, he promised not to say anything about Rick and me."

"Where did Nate spot you with Charlie?" I asked.

"Why is that important?"

I had an idea, but I didn't want to say anything just yet. "Come on, Rose, I need to know."

"We were leaving my shop one night, and Nate was sitting on the bench in front of my place along the brook. Why?"

"Do you remember when it was?"

Rose frowned, then said, "I'm pretty sure that it was the night before Charlie died. Why?"

Had Nate been stalking Charlie Cobb, waiting for a chance to exact his revenge, or was the meeting just a coincidence? "Hang on a second, Rose, I need to make a phone call."

"Go ahead and call whoever you'd like, but I'm leaving as soon as I finish packing. If you're not finished by the time I am, that's just too bad for you."

I got my phone out of my purse and dialed Sandy's number. Why hadn't I thought to check that out before? She answered on the fourth ring.

"Sandy, it's Carolyn. I need a favor."

She said softly, "I'd love to help, but I'm in the middle of something right now."

"This can't wait," I said.

"Hang on a second." After two minutes, Sandy came back on the line. "Carolyn, I hope this really is important, because I'd hate to get fired for blowing my boss off like that."

"I wouldn't have asked you otherwise. Do you keep records of who checks out the microfiche?"

"Yes, but that's near my desk, so if anyone used it, I'd know about it. Besides, I've got the key, remember?"

"This is important. Has Nate Walker been by there in the past two weeks?"

Sandy paused, then said, "No, I thought of that, but I can't remember him ever visiting the library, at least not that department."

"But you don't work all the time, do you? Would you check your log? I'll hold."

As I waited for Sandy to come back on the line, I watched Rose haul another armload of personal things to her car. It appeared that she was absolutely serious about leaving town. I'd feel horrid if I was the cause of it, but I'd have to look at it as collateral damage. Bill's reputation was at stake, maybe even his life, and our ability to keep living in Maple Ridge was on the line, even if Sheriff Hodges decided not to arrest him for murder. Tongues would keep wagging and people would keep speculating, regardless of the truth.

Rose waved a final farewell to me, and I called out, "Where are you going?"

"I don't know yet."

"Are you coming back?"

"I sincerely doubt it."

Before I could ask her anything else, she

was gone. I hated to see her leave, but now that she wasn't my prime suspect, I could hardly throw myself in front of her car to stop her.

Sandy came back on the line. "Sorry I took so long. You're right. He came by one night I wasn't working."

"Check the date."

I held my breath as she said, "It was two nights before Charlie Cobb was murdered."

That was half my theory proven, and now it was time for the other half. "Does the log give the dates of the material he checked out?"

There was silence on the other end, then Sandy said, "It was the same time frame I looked up myself later. He was reading the newspapers for the month after his wife died."

"So he saw Charlie's DUI arrest before the man was murdered?"

"He had to," Sandy said. "Carolyn, I'm so sorry. I just assumed I'd know if he'd been by."

"It's not your fault. You can't be there every hour the library's open. You deserve a life, too, you know."

"What are you going to do? Do you really think he's guilty?"

"I'm pretty sure of it. Now all I have to

do is get the proof I need."

She hesitated, then asked, "You're not going to confront Nate by yourself, are you?"

"No, I'm not that crazy. After we hang up, I'm calling the sheriff and telling him what I found out. He might ridicule me for snooping, but he's got to check it out. I'd expect his visit in about an hour, if everything goes according to plan."

"Call him as soon as we hang up," Sandy said as my telephone started beeping. Blast it, I'd forgotten to recharge it yet again. "Sandy," I started to say, hoping to get her to call the sheriff for me, but my telephone died before I could finish. I wasn't going to be able to call Hodges, but I wasn't that far from his office. Maybe that was best anyway. At least if I talked to him face-to-face, he couldn't hang up on me.

I got into the Intrigue and had just put the keys in the ignition when I heard a voice behind me. "You just couldn't stop snooping, could you, Carolyn?"

I didn't have to turn around to know that Nate Walker was sitting behind me. I felt a nudge in my neck as the knife in his hand tweaked me.

CHAPTER 13

I could feel a trickle of blood run down my neck. "Ouch. That hurt," I said. "What do you think you're doing?"

"Don't play coy with me. I heard your entire conversation with that nosy librarian. You couldn't just leave it alone, could you? I had a feeling you'd finally twig to what I did. I've been following you around town for days. The sheriff was never a threat. If it makes you feel any better, you were the only one I was worried about. After I take care of you, that librarian is going to have an accident herself. You were too smart for your own good."

I wasn't sure if I should be flattered, but at the moment all I could think about was the knife still pressed against my neck. I started to dab at the blood with a tissue, but Nate snapped, "Don't do anything stupid."

"If blood gets on my blouse, it'll ruin it."

Why on earth had I said that? It was the craziest thing in the world to complain about at the moment.

Nate wasn't amused. "If you don't do exactly what I say, it's going to get a lot more blood on it. Start the car."

I kept my hands in my lap. "I need to know where we're going first."

He said, "Do you really want me to cut you again?"

"Take it easy. I'm going." I started the Intrigue, but I kept it in park.

Nate snapped, "What are you waiting for?"

"I still need a direction."

He paused a minute, then said, "Take Compton Road out of town. And don't try anything, Carolyn. This knife might slip and go in a little farther."

"I'll do what you say," I said as I started driving. Compton led out of town straight into the woods. There were too many places Nate could kill me and leave my body, and it would take the sheriff forever to find me. I couldn't afford to let things get that far. I knew I was a goner if I listened to everything Nate said, and surprisingly, that helped. After all, if I was going to die anyway, which was starting to look like a near certainty, I might as well take him out, too, if I could manage it. I was sorry I wouldn't be able to say good-bye to my husband or my two sons, but I hoped they'd be proud that I'd died fighting.

"Slow down," he ordered. I wanted to mash the accelerator to the floor, but we were going through downtown, and there were people out shopping, enjoying the day, oblivious to the drama unfolding in my car. It was too risky to try anything just yet. I didn't mind the thought of taking Nate out with me, but knowing I had hurt an innocent bystander would be too much to live with, even if only for a few seconds.

I asked softly, "How did you finally figure out that Charlie was probably the one who killed your wife?"

"I've been struggling to put Winnie's death out of my mind since she died, but you and those two biddies brought it all to light again. I've never stopped thinking about how she died, but I suddenly realized I hadn't approached the problem very systematically. I was in some kind of a haze that just wouldn't lift. That's when I thought about searching through old newspapers to see if there was anything that might be related to what happened to her that night. Charlie Cobb's DUI stood out."

"The sheriff must have suspected the same thing," I said.

"There was something that wasn't in the papers. Evidently Charlie got a girlfriend to lie about his whereabouts that night, and Hodges bought it."

"How do you know that?" I asked, glancing back at Nate in the rearview mirror. I almost wished I hadn't. His eyes were black and empty, as if Nate's soul had already left his body.

"Charlie told me everything just before he died."

I hadn't even considered the possibility that Charlie Cobb had actually talked to his murderer before he died. "So you didn't just sneak up on him and hit him with that brick?"

"Give me some credit, Carolyn. I had a suspicion but no proof. I decided to talk to Charlie, to hear what he had to say for himself. The fool broke down crying, if you can believe that. He said he's been waiting since it happened for that tap on the shoulder. He was almost relieved that he didn't have to hide it anymore."

"So you killed him," I said.

"What was I supposed to do? Take him to Hodges and have him confess again? Where did that leave me? Knowing the sheriff, he'd botch the arrest and Charlie would go free. No, Winnie's blood cried out for vengeance, and it was my job to give it."

The foot traffic was thinning out, and I was almost ready to make my move. I had to stall him for a few more minutes, then I'd be ready to take my shot at wrecking the car. I had my seat belt on, but from the way Nate was kneeling against the back of my seat, I knew he wasn't belted in. If I could throw him through the windshield, I might be able to get away, and if he died in the process, I would try not to lose any sleep over it.

"I didn't know your wife, but I heard she had a good heart. Would she have wanted you to commit murder, for any reason?"

"Don't talk about Winnie," he said, drawing fresh blood. "You're not worthy."

"Sorry," I said.

It was time. I glanced in my rearview mirror, and though nobody was following us, I said, "There's the sheriff. He's right behind us. What do you want me to do?"

Nate looked over his shoulder, and the pressure eased off my neck for just a moment. Against every instinct I had, I jerked the car into a telephone pole and hit it square on.

The air bag deployed in my face, and I felt a thud behind me. As the bag collapsed, I reached for my seat belt and stumbled out of the Intrigue, straight into Butch's arms.

"Are you all right?" he asked me. "You're bleeding. You must have cut yourself."

"He did that," I said as I tried to look into the back of the car. There was blood on the backseat window, and I realized that I'd probably killed Nate in the collision.

Butch yanked the door open, and the coffee shop owner tumbled out onto the ground.

"Is he dead?" I asked.

Butch checked for a pulse, but judging by the blood on Nate's face, I didn't expect he would find one.

Butch grinned at me instead. "His heartbeat is strong. Nate's going to have a whale of a headache when he comes to, but my guess is that he's going to be fine."

I couldn't believe it. "But what about all that blood?"

"If I had to guess, I'd say that you broke his nose, and maybe another bone or two, but he'll survive."

There was a faint siren in the background. "Did you call the sheriff?"

Butch grinned. "He wasn't happy about it, but I finally got him on board."

"How did you know where to find me?" My head was spinning, and I wanted to lean against something, so I backed up against the car. Bill had ordered that Intrigue for me special, and now I'd wrecked it. Even if it could be repaired, I didn't ever want to drive it again. I'd never be able to sit in the driver's seat without remembering the bite of that knife on my neck.

"I was looking for you at Fire at Will and I saw you drive by. Nate was crouched down, but I could see that someone was behind you. I nearly broke my arm getting into my car. I was about to ram you myself when you wrecked. That was a nice bit of driving, by the way."

"I don't know about that. I was just happy to have a seat belt and an air bag."

Butch nudged Nate with a toe, and he groaned slightly. "I'm just as glad he didn't."

Hodges pulled up, and Butch and I quickly brought him up-to-date. There was no scolding in the man's voice as he said, "An ambulance is right behind me."

"Butch said he isn't hurt too much," I said, looking down at Nate.

"It's for you. Did you even realize you were bleeding?"

I put my hand to my neck and saw quite a bit more blood than I'd expected. For some odd reason, the sight of it made me woozy. "I'm all right."

Butch shook his head. "We've got an iron

woman on our hands."

The ambulance arrived, and the techs started for Nate.

The sheriff said, "He can wait. See to her first."

One of them obliged, while the other started ministering to Nate. I was led to the back of the ambulance, and in a minute the wounds were cleaned and bandages applied. "Thanks," I said.

"You still need to go to the ER," the EMT said, "but that should hold you for now."

Sandy drove up, with Bill in the passenger seat. As soon as he got out of the car, I collapsed into his arms, but all I could say was, "I wrecked that beautiful car you gave me."

Bill stroked my hair gently. "That doesn't matter. We can have it fixed good as new."

"I don't want it. Not now. Not ever."

"Fine. Whatever you say. I'm just happy you're all right."

"Me, too."

I looked over and saw that they were loading Nate onto a stretcher. He was coming around, but he wasn't making that much sense. "Is it worse than we thought?" I asked.

Hodges said, "No, but they like to take precautions. Do you want to ride to the hospital with us?" he said as he pointed to the ambulance.

"We'll see that she gets there," Butch said.

The sheriff didn't challenge it, and we followed the ambulance in Butch's car, with Sandy right behind us.

Bill asked softly, "Why didn't you call me?"

"I tried, but you must have been working in your shop."

"I'll never forgive myself that I wasn't there for you," Bill said.

Butch shook his head. "There wasn't anything anybody could do. Carolyn handled it."

"By destroying my beautiful car," I said. My neck was getting sore, whether from the knife pricks or the impact of the wreck, I couldn't say.

"Enough about the Intrigue. It's metal and plastic, and it can be replaced in a heartbeat. I can't believe Nate tried to kill you."

"I don't think he's in his right mind," I said. "Killing Charlie pushed him over the edge, and I don't know how he held it together as long as he did. I owe a few folks around town an apology," I added.

"They'll understand, once they hear what really happened. By the way, what really happened?"

I grinned in spite of my pain. "It's a long story, and it looks like we're here."

Butch pulled into the ER entrance, and a husky young male nurse was waiting for me with a wheelchair.

"I can walk," I said.

"Ma'am, please take a seat. I have my orders."

There must have been some fire left in my eyes, because Butch said, "I'd rethink that if I were you."

He started to say something when Bill chimed in. "Just sit in the chair, Carolyn. Don't be such a stubborn mule about it."

I thought about chiding my husband, but I just didn't feel up to it. I plopped down in the chair, then turned to the nurse and said, "I'm Carolyn, and if I hear one more 'ma'am' out of you, you're going to be the one who needs a ride."

Bill laughed, then said, "She's going to be fine."

Butch added, "There was never any doubt in my mind."

I didn't need stitches, a good thing, since I'd hated needles since childhood. But my joy was cut short when I found out I had to get a tetanus booster shot because of the knife wounds.

As we were leaving, Sheriff Hodges approached. "Do you have a second?"

"There's no need to apologize, Sheriff," I said.

He looked startled by my comment. "Apologize? You nearly got yourself killed meddling in police business, and you actually thought I came over to say I'm sorry?"

I touched his shoulder lightly. "There's no need to gush. You're forgiven, and you're most welcome, too."

"For what?" I honestly thought his head was about to explode.

"For solving two crimes in a single day. Charlie Cobb ran down Winnie Walker, and Nate killed Charlie for it fifteen years later. Now if you'll excuse me, the pain pills they gave me are kicking in, and I've got to go home so I can get some rest."

I left him standing in the hallway of the emergency room, his mouth wide open.

That sight was almost worth the pain of getting stabbed and the price of wrecking my car.

CHAPTER 14

Two weeks later, Fire at Will was having a private party, and I was surprised to find that I was the guest of honor. The entire Firing Squad was there, along with Hannah and her son, though David was an honorary member now. Bill was lumbering around in the background, trying not to hover, and failing miserably at it, while my two sons had made a special trip home to celebrate with us.

I picked up one of the frogs in the display window and said to David, "I love these little guys, and I was right. They're selling really well."

"You should see the next line I have in mind," he said, his eyes positively alight. "I'm thinking about doing mythological creatures. Wouldn't you just love to see a dragon?"

"As long as it's in miniature," I said with a laugh. My neck was mostly healed, but

I'd have a small scar there for the rest of my life. It was a small enough price to pay for what I'd been through.

Hannah touched my shoulder. "How are you doing, Carolyn?"

"The nightmares are easing up, so that's something." I'd had a recurring dream in which Nate was holding a knife to my neck as I shopped for groceries, stood in line at the post office, and even weeded my garden. It was as though his image had been burned into every memory I had. The one good thing was that none of the dreams had taken place at the pottery shop, and for that I was forever thankful.

"That's good to hear." She nodded as she gestured toward my husband. "Bill's keeping pretty close tabs on you."

"I know, and as sweet as it is, it's driving me crazy. He hasn't built a single piece of furniture in two weeks." I smiled as I added, "He doesn't know it yet, but I'm sending him back to his shop tomorrow. Enough is enough."

David asked, "Any word on Nate?"

"David," Hannah said sharply.

"It's all right. The sheriff told me that he's cooperating fully, and that he's not going to put up a fight. Evidently he can live with what he's done, though I don't see how that's possible."

"So, what happens to the coffee shop?" Hannah asked.

"I don't know. I hadn't really thought about it. Why, do you want to buy it?"

"Me?" she asked as she laughed. "I don't think so."

I smiled. "Come on, I'll be your silent partner."

Hannah smiled. "Don't make promises you can't keep. You've never been silent in your life."

"There's always that," I said just as I noticed someone hovering outside the shop.

Hannah noticed my gaze. "Is something wrong?"

"It's Rose," I said as I started for the door.

Bill found my hand before I could reach it. He snapped, "What do you think you're doing?"

"I'm letting Rose in," I said. "At least I am if you'll move that hairy mitt of yours."

"I don't think so," he said. "You stay right here. I'll go get her."

"Bill Emerson, you're driving me crazy with this hovering. I love you with all my heart, but give me some space to breathe."

"Sorry. I was just trying to look out for you," he said.

I'd clearly hurt his feelings, so I leaned

forward and kissed his cheek. "That's all right. I know you mean well. I forgive you."

Rose neared the door, and Bill — to his eternal credit — got out of my way so I could open it.

She stood outside and said, "I don't want to interrupt your party, but I just wanted to come by to tell you I'm glad you're okay."

"Come on in and join us," I said.

"No, I don't want to interrupt. I'll talk to you tomorrow."

"Does that mean you're back?" I asked. The last time I'd seen her, she'd threatened to leave forever.

Rose shrugged. "What can I say? This is home, for better or for worse."

I hugged her. "I couldn't agree with you more."

After she was gone, I turned to look at my family and friends. My sons were studying the kilns like they were part of a science project. Butch and Jenna were in deep conversation, while Sandy and Martha were studying the small animals David had been making. I had a feeling that we'd be having a Firing Squad meeting to make them soon, and I couldn't wait.

I'd gone through a lot to make Fire at Will my own, and there was no place in the world that I'd rather be, among everyone I cared about.

CLAY-CRAFTING TIPS
USING SLIP TO MAKE SCULPTED ANIMALS

Slip is nothing more than a combination of water and the clay you're using, and I like to use it when I'm making little sculpted animals as David does in the book. Polymer sculpting clay is well suited for this project. You don't need a potter's kiln for this material; you can bake it in a toaster oven or a regular oven. The sculpting clay is readily available at craft stores, comes in lots of colors, and when baked, becomes extremely hard.

To make the frog that David makes, take enough green polymer clay — the Sculpey brand, for example — and knead it into a ball a little bigger than a quarter in diameter. Once you've got a ball, it's time to add details. To make the eyes, use white clay to form two smaller balls the size of the pad of your little finger, then score the backs of each ball with crisscrossing lines that barely scrape the surfaces. Score the body as well

295

in the location where you're going to mount the eyes, then take a dab of water on your fingertip and rub the clay until there's a wet sheen on the scored areas. Believe it or not, you've just made your own slip. Press the eyes firmly onto the body, then form up the green clay behind them until the backs of the white balls are covered and molded to the body. Using black clay, make small balls to act as the pupils, then flatten them and attach them by scoring and creating slip with water on both surfaces. There should be areas of the white exposed, with a good covering of black.

Your frog is now starting to take shape. Roll two small pieces of the green clay into stubby cylinders, then attach them to the bottom of the frog by scoring the materials and rubbing water into the grooves until slip is formed. Press them into place and then mold them until you're satisfied with their shape.

Taking a small awl, you can carve two nostrils and a smile into the body, or you can make these out of clay as well. To finish your frog, roll three or four small balls of brown clay and press them onto the frog's back to give him spots of character. Make sure everything is just how you'd like it, then bake the clay per the instructions on the box.

With a little imagination, you can create an entire menagerie of clay frogs, snakes, squirrels, and even dogs. They're great fun to make, and kids love to get them as gifts, as well as make them themselves.

We hope you have enjoyed this Large Print book. Other Thorndike, Wheeler, Kennebec, and Chivers Press Large Print books are available at your library or directly from the publishers.

For information about current and upcoming titles, please call or write, without obligation, to:

Publisher
Thorndike Press
295 Kennedy Memorial Drive
Waterville, ME 04901
Tel. (800) 223-1244

or visit our Web site at:

http://gale.cengage.com/thorndike

OR

Chivers Large Print
published by BBC Audiobooks Ltd
St James House, The Square
Lower Bristol Road
Bath BA2 3SB
England
Tel. +44(0) 800 136919
email: bbcaudiobooks@bbc.co.uk
www.bbcaudiobooks.co.uk

All our Large Print titles are designed for easy reading, and all our books are made to last.